LISA M. STACKPOLE

LACEY HONEYCUT'S HILARIOUS DISASTROUS FURRY SUMMER VACATION

Smart Kids VS. Dangerous Dummies

First published by Big Ink Publishing 2019

Copyright © 2019 by Lisa M. Stackpole

All rights reserved. No part of this publication may be reproduced, stored or transmitted in any form or by any means, electronic, mechanical, photocopying, recording, scanning, or otherwise without written permission from the publisher. It is illegal to copy this book, post it to a website, or distribute it by any other means without permission.

This novel is entirely a work of fiction. The names, characters and incidents portrayed in it are the work of the author's imagination. Any resemblance to actual persons, living or dead, events or localities is entirely coincidental.

Lisa M. Stackpole asserts the moral right to be identified as the author of this work.

Lisa M. Stackpole has no responsibility for the persistence or accuracy of URLs for external or third-party Internet Websites referred to in this publication and does not guarantee that any content on such Websites is, or will remain, accurate or appropriate.

Designations used by companies to distinguish their products are often claimed as trademarks. All brand names and product names used in this book and on its cover are trade names, service marks, trademarks and registered trademarks of their respective owners. The publishers and the book are not associated with any product or vendor mentioned in this book. None of the companies referenced within the book have endorsed the book.

First edition

ISBN: 978-1-7343809-0-3

This book was professionally typeset on Reedsy. Find out more at reedsy.com

Contents

Acknowledgement	v
INVISIBLE CHILDREN	1
SOGGY SALUTE	9
TERRIBLY GREAT	14
FLYING OATHS	19
CRITTER COMMUNICATIONS	23
JOB OVERLOAD	30
THREE BRAINS	32
TAWKY SKEWL	36
DEER ME	40
STINK WARS	45
MUNCHKIN WHISPERS	49
STINKY INTERROGATION	53
WIGGLES WORLD	55
STINKY SAD	61
SKYPE DANCING	65
LACEY'S ROOM	69
EVIL SHADOW	75
EVIL SOLUTIONS	80
EVIL SPIES	86
CONFUSING CONFESSION	90
MARSHMALLOW WINNER	96
SCOOBY MYSTERY	99
ARRESTING DEVELOPMENTS	103

NAKED BOOGER	107
BOOGER PROBLEMS	111
EXPLODING ARREST	115
HORSING AROUND	119
BOOGER SOLUTIONS	122
TUFF LOVE	126
LACEY'S MISSING	130
BIRTHDAY SPIES	133
GLOWING CONTESTANTS	137
TWERP WARS	143
BOOGER SOLUTIONS	150
FLYING CURLERS	154
ALIEN BABY	160
MINUSCULE VISITOR	164
BLUE SHOCK	169
HAT DANCING	174
SPY PLANS	178
FLAMING GIRLS	181
DIGITTY DAWGALICIOUS	185
BAD MONKEY	191
THE WATCHERS	197
BATTLE PLANS	201
SLIPPERY SITUATION	206
PARTY PLANS	213
PARTY SURPRISE	216
PARTY POOPER	221
About the Author	235
Also by Lisa M. Stackpole	236

Acknowledgement

Thank you to all the playful and wonderful children in my life who constantly begged me to "Tell us another funny pet story!" Lacey Honeycut is for you!

Love and appreciation for my pet sitting clients. Your animals are part of my extended family. You may recognize some of them in this book.

Amy Sulista, you took my ideas and turned them into adorable and hilarious illustrations. I hope you'll stay with Lacey and her gang for all of our exciting adventures to come! A round of applause for my beta-reading team who provided invaluable feedback in the first round of editing. Lisa Nix, endless gratitude for listening to my ramblings and providing unfettered positive feedback. Joey Green, your background in humor and middle-grade writing gave me the ah-ha moment the book needed.

Most of all, thank you to the Lacey Honeycut readers. You are the reason I share her stories. Join the Yay-Cationers Fan Club by following Lacey, Maxwell, Anna and Mickey on Instagram and YouTube as they turn every vacation into a Yay-Cation!

Lacey Honeycut's
Hilarious Disastrous Furry Summer Vacation

SMART KIDS
VS
DANGEROUS DUMMIES

LISA M. STACKPOLE

1

INVISIBLE CHILDREN

Eleven-year-old, Lacey Honeycut, coasted hands-free, on her lavender bicycle. She sang the song, *School's out for Summer* at the top of her lungs. As Lacey pulled into the driveway of the community pool, her nostrils fluttered with glee.

Ah sunscreen, the coconutty smell of summer!

Lacey parked next to the full bicycle rack and tossed one of her light-brown, braided piggy tails behind her shoulder. As she got off her bike, she noticed that she was wearing two different color flip-flops—neither of them matched her new blue and yellow bathing suit.

Mis-matched again. Oh, well, too late now. I'm here—and anyway, who cares? It's the first day of summer vacation! I don't think the fashion police will get me.

She kept her backpack on with its wiggling passenger and grabbed her towel from the bike basket.

It's hotter than a firecracker out. I'm ready for cold water and our summer kick-off party!

Lacey moved her sunglasses to her head. Her gray-blue eyes scanned the crowded patio area looking for her best friends

Anna and Maxwell as she continued singing.

I hope they saved a chair for me at the table.

Lacey made her way into the crowd. Shady Pines was a typical neighborhood pool. She scooted past a typical grandpa sitting in the shade reading a book. She walked around a typical mom smearing gooey, white sunblock all over her kid's face. Lacey yelled, "Hey! Watch out!" to a typical rowdy kid who almost knocked her over on his cannonball-run approach. She spied a typical toddler wearing floaties and crying in the baby pool.

I don't see Anna and Maxwell.

Lacey stopped between the baby pool and lounge chairs full of people. Her path was blocked by a typical older woman dressed like a decorated three-star-admiral, with long, white gloves, wearing a sailor's hat, holding a stack of pamphlets in one hand and a white umbrella that read, "Neighborhood Watch Committee" over her head in the other.

THAT is definitely not typical.

The out-of-place admiral wore a stiffly starched white shirt with gold and silver marine epaulets on the shoulders. Colorful patches covered her shirt like military medals but they said things like, "Best Community Safety Leader" and "I'm a blood donor!". Her white dress pants were ironed with perfect pleats. Tall, white socks peered out from her white sandals. A blue scarf with little white anchors sat below her short, curly gray hair and a sailor's hat tipped to one side on her head. Sweat was pouring down the side of her face and the yummy aroma of coconut lotion was replaced by stink-o-rama.

Pew! Is she in the military? Why the umbrella? What-da-what-da? What is she doing here? Why is she covered from head to toe when it's baking outside?

Lacey had so many questions. Lacey had zero answers.

Distant thunder rumbled in the sky

Wacky sailor alert! I need to dodge this woman.

Lacey lowered her head to avoid eye-contact and tried to slide past the overdressed and sweaty, Officer Stinky.

Not quick enough.

The woman's eyes locked on Lacey. She took a step to the left, completely blocking her path. She looked Lacey up and down, her eyes stopping on Lacey's mismatched flip-flops. Her eyebrows arched to form an angry-looking triangle. General Stinky pushed the pile of pamphlets in front of Lacey's face and said, "You look like you could use this."

Lacey stood frozen-in-place, frazzled and gawking at Admiral Absurd. From somewhere in a land far, far away, Lacey realized the woman's mouth was moving, and she was yakity-yakking at Lacey.

"Young lady, I'm talking to you," she said, her voice dripping with irritation. "Don't just stand there with your mouth gaping open. Are you trying to catch flies?"

"Flies?" The word shattered Lacey from her Sea Captain Stupor. "What?"

Speaking slowly as if talking to a small child, the woman said, "I told you twice to take a brochure to the table with you and commit it to memory."

Lacey stammered, "Sorry, I was just—"

The woman snapped, "Children are to be seen and not heard."

Lacey took a pamphlet from the top of the stack and looked at the cover, "Your Guide to Proper Pool Attire and Etiquette". She mumbled, "Thanks."

Still blocking her way, the woman didn't budge.

Does she expect me to read it right now?

Lacey heard Anna calling her from the other side of the pool. She leaned around the etiquette ambassador and caught sight of Anna's head popping up and down in the crowd. "Hey, Lacey, we're over here. We've got pepperoni and meatball with extra cheese for you!"

Lacey said, "Excuse me, my friend is calling me."

With a heavy sigh, the woman stepped aside.

Geezy mageezy, that was weird.

Lacey made her way over to the table on the other side of the pool. Still shocked by the weird woman's behavior, she took a seat between Maxwell and Anna. Maxwell's strawberry blonde hair was wet from swimming. White sun-block covered his freckled nose, and he wore his baby-blue "Cool Genius" t-shirt that matched his eyes.

Lacey chuckled to herself.

Maxwell Ayce really IS a cool genius. I don't know anyone with his brilliant brain who also dances on a competitive hip-hop street team. The boy has moves.

Maxwell acknowledged her with a wink as he focused on his current mission, stuffing an entire piece of pizza in his mouth.

Her other best friend, Anna Chuong wore a bright yellow bikini with matching sunglasses and a floppy hat covering her chin-length, black hair. Anna was Vietnamese-American and very petite. Her cute face scrunched up in complete disgust as she picked ham cubes off her salad. "This is supposed to be a veggie-delight, not a dead piggy salad." Anna was a serious vegetarian.

Lacey opened her backpack and removed a blue, wriggling mouse wearing a shirt that said "Rodents Rule". She put him on the table and gave him a piece of pizza crust. "Here you go Mickey."

Anna said, "Lacey, you know I don't like Mickey near my food."

"Don't worry; he's not fond of salads."

Mickey started gnawing on the crust while delivering his best stink-eye directly at Anna. Irritated, he put the crust down and mimicked her high-pitched girl's voice. *"You know I don't like Mickey near my food."*

He jumped in the air, pointed his finger at her and continued squealing. *"Jumping germs! You need to lighten up on your mouse-manners. Yes, I'm a common house-mouse from the Bronx, but my father raised me to be a gentleman."*

Anna said, "He sure is squealing a lot."

Mickey slapped both paws to his forehead and sat back down. *"Why am I wasting my breath? A glowing, green alien from outer space has a better chance of understanding my intelligent and witty remarks. Has anyone ever heard of a mouse that only CATS can understand? ANYONE? It must have been caused by the radiation they exposed me to at that Frankenstein laboratory Lacey rescued me from."*

Deep in thought, he stroked his whiskers with his hands.

"Cheese and crackers! I just had a terrible realization! Only cats understand what I'm saying. What if that radiation made me part CAT? That is definitely NOT something that the boys back home must ever know about."

Anna looked at Lacey, who had a mouth full of food. "Bestie are you ready for the most epic summer ever?"

Lacey flashed Anna thumbs-up.

Maxwell handed her a cup of lemonade. "Slow down, slugger. There's enough for everyone."

Lacey accepted the lemonade and washed the pizza down with one gulp. "Sorry, I've been so busy with the last day of school that I forgot to eat! I'm so hungry, I could eat a horse."

Lacey quickly thought about her horse Lancelot and said, "Let me rephrase that. I'm so hungry I could eat an entire pizza!"

Anna giggled and took a bite of her salad. "No talk about eating horses."

Lacey motioned for Maxwell and Anna to lean in close so she could whisper. They both scooted closer.

Using her inside voice, she said, "Don't turn around now, but what is the dealio with *Ms.* Admiral Whitey-Tidy lounging over there by the diving board?"

Maxwell and Anna's heads whipped around to look.

Lacey put her forehead down on the table and moaned, "I just told you both not to look."

They spied the lady sitting in a lounge chair by the pool. She was by herself reading a booklet, *Women's Society of Yachting Rules & Regulations.*

Two heads swiveled back to Lacey.

"Sorry!" Anna whispered as they re-gathered like football players in a game-changing huddle.

Lacey said, "It's like watching a train wreck."

"A yacht wreck," Maxwell laughed.

Anna placed her finger to her lips and reported in low tones, "That's Mrs. Wigglesworth. She's the president of The Honorable Society to Empower Female Women Worldwide and Across the Universe."

Lacey said, "What?"

Anna said, "Yes, I know. It sounds ridiculous and—"

Maxwell cut in. "Repetitious?"

Lacey said, "Shhhh! Let her finish."

Anna leaned in so close that her head bumped Lacey's and

whispered, "The only reason that I know this is because she goes to my mom's hair salon twice a week to get a hair trim and wash."

Lacey leaned back and burst out. "Whoa, Nelly! Twice a week! Who gets their hair cut twice a week?"

Mickey reached for more pizza crust and said, *"My mouse friend Fatso from the neighborhood used to get his hair trimmed twice a week. He said it made him look thinner."*

This time, Maxwell put his fingers to his lips. "Shhhh", let her finish.

Lacey stuck her tongue out at Maxwell.

Anna rolled her eyes. "As I was saying, she's one of my mom's most faithful salon customers. My mother told me that Mrs. Wigglesworth is the president of The Honorable Society to Empower Female Women Worldwide and Across the Universe because it's been her lifelong goal to be president of an important ladies' society—but here's the thing."

Anna's voice dropped to a bare whisper. "Mrs. Wigglesworth had to start her own business so she could elect HERSELF president. Mrs. Wigglesworth is the president and the ONLY MEMBER! She couldn't convince any other women to join her social club."

Lacey said, "Probably because she's a bully."

"Why, what happened?" asked Anna.

Lacey placed Mickey on her shoulder for a better view of the party and said, "She told me that children are to be seen and not heard."

Maxwell gave a low whistle and shook his head. "Maybe she would like us better if we were invisible?"

Anna said, "We could get her to fund our next Trias-Lab project—invisibility."

Everyone laughed.

Lacey looked at her friends, crossed her eyes, wiggled her eyebrows, and slapped her gaping chin closed with her hand. "We'll call it Project Invisible Child." Anna, Maxwell, and Mickey broke out laughing at her hilarious antics.

Anna said, "I'll get working on that project right away." A smile spread across her face. "It's click time!"

Anna had a collection of cameras and always carried one with her. Her photo-developing room was located in their Trias-Lab in Maxwell's basement. She leaped up and handed her camera to a teenager walking by, "Excuse me; Can you take a picture of me and my friends?"

The girl took the camera from her and said, "Sure." Then she said to Lacey, "Your Smurf mouse is cute."

Mickey stood up on Lacey's shoulder and shook his fist. *"SMURF MOUSE! You got a lot of nerve!"*

Anna shouted, "I'm the spunky monkey in the middle! This is our beginning of summer picture." She jumped in between Maxwell and Lacey. "Smile!"

With the pool behind them and Mickey on Lacey's shoulder, they had their first summer photo. As Anna was sitting back down, Mrs. Wigglesworth walked behind them and bumped Lacey's chair, causing Mickey to lose his balance. He fell off Lacey's shoulder and landed directly in front of Mrs. Wigglesworth who stood dumbstruck, opening and closing her mouth like a goldfish.

2

SOGGY SALUTE

Mickey had never seen a sailor before. He stood up on his hind feet to get a better look. "*Should I salute? I don't know the protocol.*"

Mrs. Wigglesworth pointed her long, gloved finger at Mickey and screamed, "A BLUE RAT!"

Mickey gasped, "*Rat? You insult me, my family and my proud Italian mouse ancestors!*"

At the sound of Mickey's loud squeaking, Mrs. Wigglesworth took a step back and lost her footing. She seemed to fall backward in slow motion with a look of complete panic plastered on her face.

SMACK!

Without composure or any sense of control, she landed flat on her back in the deep end of the pool, a sopping wet sailor without her ship.

Mickey grabbed his stomach and fell over laughing. "*That's what you get for calling me a rat! I place the Curse of the Bambino on you and your family!*"

EVERYONE at the pool stood up to get a closer look at the

floundering sailor in the pool. Lacey quickly grabbed Mickey and hid him in her pocket. The teenage lifeguard blew his whistle like a conductor on a train shouting "All Aboard!"

"Everyone out of the water!"

He dove in and tried—unsuccessfully to help Mrs. Wigglesworth who was frantically waving her arms around and trying to get to the ladder.

Lacey grabbed her bag and said, "Let's get out of here before someone reports Mickey!"

All three friends grabbed their stuff and raced to the parking lot.

Lacey said, "This way, remember our second-grade fort?"

They slid in between the missing fence pole (still broken) and scrambled over the grassy hill.

Maxwell shouted, "It's still here!"

The small lean-to made of rocks and branches and tied together with twine was still standing. There was a loud clap of thunder and it started to rain. As the rain came down hard, Anna was the last one to scoot into the dry shelter, breathless and laughing.

"I almost lost my new hat!"

Lacey was breathing hard too. She leaned back against her bag and laughed hysterically.

Maxwell said, "That was priceless! Did you see the look on her face when she yelled, BLUE RAT?"

It took a few minutes for everyone to stop laughing and start breathing again.

Finally, Lacey said, "I can't believe this fort is still here, and it's waterproof. We did a good job building it. This is the very spot where we first decided to start our lab in Maxwell's house."

Maxwell said, "Good times, third grade and look at us now. We've won awards and have a chance at getting scholarships to space camp next spring."

Lacey said, "Remember that summer after third grade when we camped out here for the night?"

Anna added, "Without telling our parents!"

Maxwell said, "It didn't take long for my detective dad to find us and order us all home before it even got dark outside."

Anna remembered, "We were having so much fun. I wanted to stay the whole night and make a fire, tell ghost stories and roast marshmallows."

Maxwell said. "Ghost stories? Banana you wouldn't have

lasted past dark. You would have gotten freaked out and cried for your Mama."

Anna retorted, "Would not!"

Lacey agreed, "Would too!"

Anna pulled her knees up and hugged them. "You're probably both right."

Lacey said, "We got in so much trouble, but we had some fun times in this fort."

Mickey popped his head out of Lacey's bag and looked around. "*Is the coast clear? Is the soggy-sailor lady still treading water? I sure showed her when I placed the Curse of the Bambino on her. My Grandfather mouse from Boston taught me all about the curse. It haunted the Boston Red Sox for 86 years when they traded away the Bambino, Babe Ruth. One long losing streak!*"

He climbed out and walked to the center of the fort.

Lacey said, "There's my dangerous, blue RAT!"

Mickey squared off, put his paws on his hips and narrowed his eyes at Lacey. "*Smurf mouse and blue rat, these people are more colorblind than my cousin Ralphy. Hello! For brilliant lab geeks, you can't see something that is as plain as the nose on your face! I have shiny, black fur, just like my momma had.*"

He pivoted slowly in a circle like a supermodel on the runway, arms spread wide.

"*360 degrees of glossy, black fur, finer than the most expensive mink coat at Macey's. Take a look and repeat after me, black, black, black.*"

Lacey picked up her squeaking mouse and attached him to his leash.

"Here you go, Mickey. Is that what you're squeaking about?"

Mickey inspected the leash and leered at Lacey.

"Gee, thanks. Your trust in me is inspiring. Cocker Spaniels get more respect."

He sat down to pout and glumly groomed himself.

Anna reached into her pocket. "I think I've got a cracker in here for him."

A folded-up note fell onto the ground.

Anna handed it to Lacey.

"SORRY! I knew there was something important that I forgot to tell you. Charlotte gave me this note in our last class today and said it was urgent that I give it to you."

Charlotte was a champion competitor in the Junior Paralympics horse-riding events and one of Lacey's best horse-riding friends.

Lacey asked, "Urgent? What else did she say?"

Anna grimaced. "She may have said it's a matter-of-life-and-death."

Lacey said, "ANNA!" and grabbed the note. She unfolded it and read it out loud.

"Lacey, I'm in big trouble! Meet me at Huntclub after school!"

3

TERRIBLY GREAT

Lacey was practically flying in the rain on her lavender bike. It was an Electra girl's cruiser with wide handlebars and a comfy seat—a Christmas present delivered from her dad in California. The lavender Electra was a complete surprise last year. The doorbell rang, she opened the door, and there it was with a huge purple bow. The banner wrapped around it read *Merry Christmas Elfie, Love Dad.* Lacey's dad nicknamed her Elfie because she was born on Christmas Eve. Lacey always wore the tiny Elfie charm necklace her dad gave her when he told her that her parents were getting divorced.

As she entered the stables on the muddy dirt road, she shot her foot back, engaging the brakes. This sent her into a sideways skid. In all her excitement, Lacey had misjudged her approach speed and the mud factor.

She shouted, "Whoa Nelly!" and dragged both flip-flops in the muddy puddles to slow her approach. She barely missed crashing into Charlotte, who was in front of her horse's stall pacing nervously.

Crash averted, she said, "Charlotte, I got here as fast as I could."

Charlotte was wringing her hands. "Lacey, we have to talk. I need your help!"

Charlotte was a beautiful girl. She had two prosthetic legs from the knee down because she was born without the bottom part of her legs. She didn't let anything slow her down. Today she had her riding clothes on and boots, so you couldn't see her specially made artificial legs. Her long, white-blonde hair was down and framed her round, pale face. Her blue eyes looked very serious. Charlotte's lips quivered, and a tear rolled down her cheek.

Lacey gave her a hug. "Charlotte, what's wrong? Don't worry Whatever it is, I can help you."

Charlotte pulled back and looked at Lacey. She said, "Lacey, it's terrible. My mother came to school this morning and told me they accepted me to the Cardiff Riding School in Wales."

"That's not terrible. Charlotte, that's great!"

"Yes, it's great—but it's terrible!"

"Why?"

"Wales! Great Britain! Far Away! I will be there for two months!"

"You'll be fine. Are you worried about being homesick?"

"No, my mother grew up there. My Uncle Conway lives nearby so I can stay with him."

Lacey wiped the tear from Charlotte's cheek.

"That sounds great."

"It is great. They only award the scholarship to two riders each summer from the United States. There was a cancellation and I am the backup choice."

"And why is that not great?"

"Here's why it's not great."

She took Lacey's hand and pulled her closer to the stall. Her horse Juniper was hanging its head over the stall. Charlotte put her arms around Juniper's gray speckled head and looked at Lacey pitifully.

"Mrs. Goodall said she will have the staff feed Juniper while I'm away, but who will ride her? She has to get her exercise and practice her show routines."

Lacey sighed. "Charlotte is that all you're worried about? Seriously? That's no big deal. I can find time to ride her for you this summer."

Charlotte smiled brightly. "Would you Lacey?"

Lacey walked closer and let Juniper sniff her hand.

"Of course. You know I love Juniper almost as much as Sir Lancelot."

Charlotte said, "Lacey, there's one more reason it's not great. Who will run Charlotte's Critters while I'm gone?"

"Charlotte's Critters?"

"Lacey, you know Charlotte's Critters is the name of my neighborhood pet-sitting and dog-walking business."

"Oh, that's right."

"All those animals and their owners are counting on me."

Charlotte's eyes began to tear up again and her bottom lip was doing the Macarena.

"I won't be able to go. This horse-riding scholarship is a once-in-a-lifetime chance. Why didn't I think of this sooner? I guess I didn't expect to get chosen as the backup. My flight leaves tomorrow. What am I going to do?"

Charlotte's big blue eyes looked at Lacey.

Lacey's big blue eyes looked at Charlotte.

Lacey was a hopeless rescuer and a natural-born helper—sometimes this got her in trouble. This was one of those sometimes. Lacey didn't think about her summer plans. She made an impulsive decision. This decision would be a Lacey thing. She would help a friend. She would speak before thinking. She would make a commitment—and Lacey honored her commitments.

"Charlotte, I can take over for you while you're gone."

Charlotte started jumping up and down.

"Really? Really? Lacey Honeycut, you are my hero!"

Overwhelmed by the new hero label, Lacey gave a fist-pump and shouted out, "Lacey to the rescue!"

She looked at Charlotte, who was still jumping up and down. That's when it hit her.

"Charlotte, you played me good, didn't you?"

Charlotte flashed a wide grin and admitted, "Like a piano."

Then her face got serious again. "Lacey, it might be more complicated than you think."

4

FLYING OATHS

The next morning, Lacey rode in the car with Charlotte and her parents to the airport.

Charlotte will be gone for eight whole weeks. Almost the entire summer vacation.

Lacey was thrilled for her friend, but she would miss her. They always had fun together horsing around.

They parked in short-term parking. Thank goodness it was close because Charlotte was not a light packer.

How did the girl pack so much stuff with only one night's notice?

It was kind of impressive. It took all of them to carry her multiple suitcases and travel bags. When they got to the gate marked 2B, British Airways, passengers were already boarding the plane.

Charlotte hugged her mom tight. Her mom handed her a small paper bag. "Here's a special snack for you on the plane. Uncle Conway will meet you at the airport. We're expecting a postcard from you every week. Please try to write legibly for once!" Blinking back tears, she said, "I miss you already!"

Charlotte's dad gave her a big bear hug. "We're so proud of

you."

Charlotte picked up a shaggy pink knapsack and turned to face Lacey. On the outside, in big block letters, it read *Charlotte's Critters*. With an authoritative look on her face, she said, "Lacey, in this bag is everything you need to run Charlotte's Critters while I'm away. There are small things that you may need on visits and a large lanyard key-holder with my clients' keys to their homes. Keep this on your neck so you never accidentally lock yourself out. There's also a map showing each location marked with an X and the corresponding key number. My file book has a pet information form for each client. Pay attention to the special notes I've written on each pet file. These notes are crucial."

Lacey reached for the backpack, but Charlotte pulled it away and dangled it just out of her reach. "Uh-uh, not so fast. Hold your horses, young lady. Lacey Honeycut, raise your right hand and repeat after me."

Lacey looked puzzled. "Um—what's this?"

With a solemn face, Charlotte said, "Lacey, I'm trusting you with my pet business. I need to administer Charlotte's Oath before I turn this over to you."

A woman's voice announced, "Gate 2B, British Airways is now boarding."

Lacey joked, "Can't I just cross my heart and hope to die? Stick a needle in my eye?"

"No."

Lacey thought, *this is very Daffy Duck, but if I don't do it, she'll miss her plane.*

Lacey raised her right hand.

Charlotte said, "Repeat after me. I, Lacey Honeycut, do solemnly swear."

Lacey rolled her eyes and repeated in a high-pitched, sing-song voice, "I, Lacey Honeycut do solemnly swear."

Charlotte lifted the pink backpack even higher in the air and scolded, "Lacey, this is serious."

Lacey straightened up her posture, pushed her shoulders back and saluted. "Okay, sorry ma'am, please continue."

Charlotte said, "to take care of and protect all of Charlotte's Critters."

Lacey repeated, "to take care of and protect all of Charlotte's Critters."

Charlotte said, "in all circumstances and situations."

The woman's voice warned, "Last call for Boarding."

Charlotte's dad warned, "Charlotte, get on that plane before you miss it."

Lacey quickly repeated, "in all circumstances and situations," then yanked the backpack away from Charlotte.

Lacey Honeycut had spent her whole life preparing for this job—or any job that involved critters. The entirety of her existence was about animals. She had read every book, watched every show, and learned about animals her whole life. She even volunteered at an animal hospital. The girl *LOVED* animals! Lacey Honeycut, DVM would be her official title when she graduated from veterinary school. With a wide grin on her face, she looked Charlotte in the eyes and said, "Charlotte, I was born to do this job!"

As Charlotte moved to give her ticket to the agent, she turned back to Lacey and said, "There are a few things I forgot to warn you about."

The announcement boomed. "Final call for boarding."

Charlotte said, "I don't have time to tell you now. Just be careful."

Charlotte was about to disappear through the doorway. "It's very expensive to call Great Britain. My uncle says that most of the time, the phones don't work at the school. Just rely on the file notes and you should be okay." And then she was gone.

What did she need to warn me about?

5

CRITTER COMMUNICATIONS

After saying farewell to Charlotte at the airport, Charlotte's parents gave Lacey a ride home. Today was the official first day of summer break and she didn't want to think about Charlottes' warnings. There wasn't a cloud in the sky. It was a good day to be eleven-years-old. Life was good! Whatever the problem was, Lacey Honeycut could fix it.

Her mom's station wagon was parked in the driveway with "Baby on Board" and "Be Happy, Start a Garden" magnets on the bumper. She entered through the garage.

I'll look inside Charlotte's bag later. She dropped the pink furry bag on the kitchen floor and ran up the stairs two steps-at-a-time.

Mickey was running along the wall in his custom-made tunnel system. His training to perform search and rescue tasks was going well. By entering small spaces, the tiniest rescue animal ever trained, could accomplish things that larger animals could not, Project Mickey was top secret. He was getting his aerobic workout this morning, wearing a shirt that said "Muscle Mouse" and running the tunnels.

Mickey looked at his reflection as he passed a window. "*I almost feel sorry for all the single and sassy girl mice. How could they possibly resist all this! Good looks, brains, and muscles. This mouse is the total package. I'm a hunk-a-hunk of burning love! I'll be ready for professional mouse boxing soon enough. My father always said I should have been a boxer. By the end of this summer, I'll be ready to hitchhike my way back to New York City and hit the boxing circuit.*"

Mickey stopped running to catch his breath. He spotted Lacey.

"*Lacey's back from rescuing Charlotte at the airport. She's a good kid, but MICKEY? I mean of all the names to give me. It's not like she rescued me from Disney World. I was in an illegal lab in New York—in the Bronx. That experimental lab had terrible plans for me and I'm grateful that Lacey found out and adopted me, but did she have to name me Mickey? I can just hear my New York buddies now singing the Mickey Mouse Club song, M-I-C-K-E-Y M-O-U-S-E.*"

He shouted, "*Hey Lacey, I'm done with my training and ready for lunch.*"

Lacey pulled a few books from her bookshelves and tossed them onto her bed. Later, she would brush up on techniques and facts to help her with Charlotte's Critters.

Mickey sat next to the wheel and started doing his stretching.

Lacey's stomach growled. "I'm starving. Mickey, are you hungry?"

He climbed into her open palm and said, "*Do Penguins like to ice skate?*"

They headed to the kitchen where Drowsy was lying in her cat bed.

Lacey said, "Hello, my gorgeous kitty. How was your day?"

Drowsy gave one of her cutest meows. It was a long meow combined with a yawn. Lacey called it a meyawn.

"That exciting, huh?"

She remembered when she first brought her cat home from the animal shelter. She was so teeny-tiny. All she did was sleep. She slept in Lacey's bed, in her laundry hamper, and even curled up with Lacey's Scooby-Doo stuffed animal.

Feast your eyes on the difficult life of a cat.

When Lacey saw her that day curled up on her comforter, she came up with the name Drowsy. Since then, Drowsy had blossomed into a beautiful two-year-old white Persian cat with big blue eyes and a smooshed-up adorable face.

Mom walked into the kitchen with Lacey's baby brother Petey on her hip and pointed at the pink Charlotte's Critters bag. "Is that yours?"

"I'm taking over Charlotte's pet-sitting and dog-walking business this summer while she's in Wales. That backpack has all the files and keys and stuff."

Mom started bouncing Petey up and down.

"That sounds like a mighty big obligation. Are you sure you're ready for that?"

"Mom, I had to help her out. She was in a real bind. There's nobody better for this job. Don't worry. I got this."

"The famous last words of Lacey Honeycut."

Lacey grabbed her snack. "Very funny mom. I've got a Skype meeting scheduled with Maxwell and Anna to talk about our summer plans. I'll be in the office."

Lacey was daydreaming as she waited for the computer to boot up.

This will be an epic summer!

Her best friends had a long list of must-dos. Must-do: swim and hang out at the neighborhood pool. Must-do: ride horses at Huntclub. Must-do: finalize Top-secret Project Mickey in their science laboratory, and definitely, Must-do: the annual Fourth of July small town Meriwether Pines celebration.

Anna, Maxwell, and Lacey's shared love for invention and wacky science projects had bonded them together since first grade. Their Trias-Lab in Maxwell's basement was a place to have fun and push the envelope. Trias was Latin for trio and it became their motto, three brains, one lab.

Last summer they built a drone that looked like a cat space-ship, named *The Starcat Enterprise* and flew it all over town, until one tragic afternoon when it collided with a bird. Yes, a real bird. On that occasion of bird vs. cat—the bird won.

Lacey wanted to spend oodles of time with her favorite rental horse, Lancelot. Twice a week, she worked at Huntclub Stables mucking out horse stalls and kept the tack room clean, in exchange for free lessons.

The Skype call connected, and Maxwell kicked off the meeting, reviewing summer projects.

Mickey was half-listening and half-snoozing on the desk.

"More boring summer plans. How about a one-way bus ticket back to New York?"

Lacey told Anna and Maxwell, "I have some interesting results to share with you about Mickey's command-recall abilities. I think he's almost ready for space camp."

Mickey jumped onto his hind legs and cupped his hands around his mouth for added sound projection. *"Now, here this. I will go to space camp when pigs fly—ain't-gonna-happen, no dice. I'll be saying Adios by then—back with my boys in the Bronx, exploring garbage cans, scaring tourists and impressing the ladies with my professional boxing moves. And for the umpteen thousandth time, MY NAME IS NOT MICKEY MOUSE! It's Antonio which means worthy of admiration, so chew on that!"*

Anna said, "He sure is squeaking a lot today. I can't wait to see him in a tiny mouse space suit. That would be hilarious!"

Mickey hollered, *"Here's a mouse-a-mathical equation. Mouse plus space equals not going to happen!"*

Anna continued, "This summer I want to shoot some videos of Mickey on a search and rescue simulation."

Lacey said, "Great idea Anna, but don't post it on our YouTube channel, it's still top secret."

Mickey brightened., *"Now we're talking hero time. Search and rescue is a definite way to impress cute lady mice. I suggest throwing in a firetruck and mouse fireman suit for maximum masculinity."*

Maxwell said, "I've started work on the mouse translation software, recording and analyzing Mickey's different mouse noises for repetitive sounds and meaning."

Mickey shouted, *"Cheese and crackers! Try listening in English! I'm not speaking Swahili!"*

When they were wrapping up, Anna said, "We heard about Charlotte's scholarship trip. I guess it's just the three musketeers this summer. I can't believe she's spending her summer in Great Britain. She's so lucky! What will happen to her pet-sitting thing while she's gone?"

"Excellent question, Anna Banana," said Maxwell. "I've seen her walking dogs in the neighborhood. It looks like a successful business."

Lacey told them the entire Lacey to the rescue story and said, "Guys, I was born to do this job!"

Anna said, "Yeah, you were!"

Maxwell asked, "Lacey, how are you going to fit in our lab time and all the other fun stuff we have planned, now that you're responsible for Charlotte's Critters?"

That's when it hit Lacey like an atom bomb.

I will be so busy helping Charlotte that I will not have time with my friends. What was I thinking?

Her lower lip shifted into a full-out pout mode and she leaned into the computer camera with sad, blue eyes. She was working it.

Maxwell took one look at Lacey's pouty face and knew he had to cheer her up. They had been best friends forever. He couldn't stand to see her sad. "Lacey, lose the pout. The banana and I will help you this summer."

6

JOB OVERLOAD

When she came down to the kitchen, Mom was just wrapping up the Charlotte Critter's story with Steve. "So that's how Lacey ended up with this job for the summer. She was being a good friend to Charlotte."

Mom and Dad got divorced when Lacey was six. After that, her dad moved back to his hometown of Los Angeles for work. He directed movies, commercials, and all kinds of cool productions.

Mom remarried three years later to Steve. Steve was a paleontologist. Lacey liked him. Two years ago, Steve and Mom had Petey, Lacey's little brother. So far, Lacey liked being a big sister.

Steve had a twinkle in his eye. "So, the girl who never wants to babysit her brother now has two summer jobs? Twice a week, you're covering chores at the Huntclub and now Charlotte's Critters. If I didn't know better, I'd think this was an elaborate plan to get out of babysitting Petey."

"Hahaha, very funny Stevo."

Steve smiled. "I'm proud of you. That's a really nice thing

you're doing for Charlotte."

Mom said, "I agree. I know how much you were looking forward to all your free time this summer."

As Steve was serving the lasagna at the table, he said, "That's a whopper of a commitment. Do you need any help from us?"

Lacey piled garlic bread on her plate. *Yum! Mom's garlic bread rocks! Tons of garlic butter and extra crunchy on the outside.*

She shrugged. "I'm good. If I end up in a pickle, Maxwell and Anna will help me."

Mom said, "Okay, we're here if you need us."

Maxwell was pacing in his front yard the next morning when Lacey and Anna arrived.

7

THREE BRAINS

They followed him down to their lab. A scrolling LED sign on the door looped the words "Welcome to Trias-Lab. A Mind-Blowing, Three Brain, Cranium Experiment". Maxwell's dad Marty helped them convert the entire basement into their laboratory. Marty's years as a famous genetic research scientist were over, but he still helped Maxwell from time to time. Maxwell was very close to his parents. Only Maxwell's best friends knew that he was a fraternal twin whose brother had been kidnapped at birth and was still missing. That drove his father to quit working as a scientist and become a detective. Nobody talked about it.

Trias-Lab had the appearance of a chaotic, mad scientist's secret den. One wall had metal shelves from floor to ceiling loaded with all kinds of parts, tools, batteries, cameras, wires, test tubes, lightbulbs, and more. One corner had a table with laboratory gas burners and glass tubes filled with colored liquids. Some cylinders were smoking, bubbling, or glowing iridescent colors. Anna's photo-lab closet was next to the stairs.

On the wall, a chalkboard with algorithms and calculations written hung next to a tall glass case with Maxwell's hip-hop dance troop trophies and ribbons. Maxwell proudly displayed his FAA Pilot Drone License in a frame.

The largest wall was covered with framed science awards, certificates, degrees, trophies, and framed photographs of Maxwell standing with famous smarties, astronauts, science professors, and inventors. In the center was an old black-and-white photo of Maxwell's Uncle Theo holding him as a newborn and standing next to Maxwell's mom and dad. Marty and Theo wore matching white lab coats.

Schematic renderings of Maxwell's robots R1, R2, and R3 hung by a photo of a huge trophy shaped like a rocket. The photograph had a giant red X drawn across it. The label under the picture read "Einstein Albert Wernher, Academy of Future Astronauts of America, Galaxy Explorer of the Year". Einstein was Maxwell's sworn enemy and never let anyone photograph him—even when he beat out Maxwell for Explorer of the Year.

Lacey's section of the lab was on the far wall next to the big window. Various mazes and contraptions took up the area used for Mickey's training. A large 3D printer paid for with science contest winnings were being used by Lacey for her space camp contest invention.

Maxwell said, "R3, deliver training radios."

A flying drone with a square robot head and creepy fly-wing propellers swooped in and carefully placed three walky-talkies in front of Maxwell. "Training radios delivered."

Maxwell passed out the walky-talkies and said, "R3, deliver chargers."

R3 swooped over to a metal shelf, using its strange praying mantis arms to pick up three small chargers. With its red laser eyes flashing, it gingerly laid three chargers on the table. "Chargers delivered." R3 hovered silently in place, waiting for further instructions.

Maxwell said, "R3, back to the base charging station."

The bizarre insect-bot silently returned to its charger and landed perfectly on the port.

Lacey shook her head. *Half the time, I don't know whether I'm impressed by Maxwell's genius IQ or creeped out by it.*

THREE BRAINS

8

TAWKY SKEWL

Anna said, "Maxwell, R3 is kind of weird."

Maxwell said, "Yup." He passed out the chargers, waist clips, and index cards with typing on both sides. "Okay, Critter Team, it's training time. Professor Maxwell is going to skewl you on walkies. Let's get serious."

Anna rolled her eyes.

"The waist clip is so you can keep the walky on you at all times. First, let's review the standard shortwave radio lingo. These police and CB radio terms are standard across the board. Use them at all times when communicating. I've prepared this small cheat note index card that you can keep with you."

Anna and Lacey listened patiently while 'Professor Maxwell' explained the meanings and uses of shortwave radio terms. They reviewed come in, over, over and out, copy that, wilco, 10-4, 10-20, roger that and mayday. Using his I'm-the-son-of-a-detective voice, Maxwell stressed that MAYDAY was only for EMERGENCIES.

Next, he showed them the back of his talky where a laminated label read, "Maxwell, mad scientist, talky #1". The girls laughed.

Maxwell smirked. "As you can see, I have taped your name, title, and correlating number on the back of your talky. My dad gave me these." He handed Lacey her walky with the label, "Lacey, I was born to do this job, walky #2".

Lacey took the two-way radio. "You know it."

Inpatient to see what Maxwell had written on her label, Anna snatched the last device from the table. She let out a pretend gasp of horror. Her tag said, "Anna Banana, talky too muchy, walky #3". She held her hand to her mouth with fake indignation and rhymed, "Well! I never met a boy so clever!"

Maxwell shrugged and pushed the red button on his walky. "Anna, this is talky #1, come in?"

They could all hear his voice over Anna's walky and in the room. Maxwell released the red button and waited for a beat.

Silence.

He looked at Anna. "Well? Push the red button and respond."

Flustered, Anna pushed the red button on her talky. "Hi Maxwell, this is your gawky walky-tawky. Please don't blocky."

Maxwell gave her a seriously disapproving frown. "Anna, state your id number and use the lingo I just taught you. You must always speak professionally in case you are on the wrong channel. Here is the most important instruction. Always keep your walky tuned into three. That will be our channel. Whatever you do, don't put it on thirty-three. That would broadcast to all emergency stations, including my father's radio, local police, fire stations and, ambulances."

They practiced more until Lacey felt comfortable and Anna stopped rhyming. Maxwell picked up a pink baseball cap sitting on his worktable. It said "Crittercam" on the front and had a micro-camera attached to the top.

Lacey took the hat to examine it. "Maxwell, what's this?"

"Just a little something extra I threw together for you."

Anna said, "Is that one of my cameras?"

Maxwell nodded. "I hope it's okay with you that I borrowed it?"

"Of course."

He pushed a remote-control button and all the blinds lowered on the windows. "I've prepared a short video showing the view from the hat." A second button lowered a small movie screen and a video started playing.

Maxwell does nothing halfway.

The short movie titled "Maxwell Ayce Introduces the Crittercam Cap", showed various neighbors walking their dogs. Maxwell's parents had fallen victim to his movie-directing debut and starred in the clip with some really bad acting. His nine-year-old neighbor Harry was also in the film, posing as a newspaper delivery boy. When the short film ended, Maxwell pushed the remote again, the screen retracted, the blinds lifted, and it was light again in Trias-Lab. Lacey and Anna were dying to laugh but kept their faces totally serious as the lights came back on.

Maxwell beamed like he just invented electricity. "Just wear the Crittercam every time you arrive at a pet visit. It will begin recording only when you're wearing it. Take it off when you leave each visit and it will automatically power down. I have programmed the video to back up every-day into the Trias-Lab's memory cloud."

"Maxwell, I love my new hat! That's so geek squad of you. What are we going to do with the stored videos?"

Maxwell scratched his chin. "I haven't really thought that far ahead. I'll back up the video and we can decide at the end of the summer if we want to use it for anything. Just remember—"

"___to put it on when I arrive and remove it when I'm done with each visit. Got it."

"Exactly, you can keep it in the Charlotte's Critters backpack. The battery is fully charged and should last all summer."

"Thanks, Maxwell!" She put the hat in the pink backpack.

Maxwell said, "Keep the walkies working by charging them every night. Turn them on every morning and keep them with you at all times. Lacey, your backup team is in place."

Lacey filled the pink backpack with all her new paraphernalia.

"I've got to go, guys. I've got my first two visits today. Thanks for backing me up. This will be easy peasy lemon squeezy! I'll call you later on the walkies. Rooby Rooby Roo!"

Lacey studied her map before she got on her bike. Ten minutes later, she looked around.

Am I going the right way?

9

DEER ME

The golf course neighborhood had rolling hills, lakes, and wildlife everywhere. A bunny hopped by and Lacey saw a young deer grazing.

I love this part of town, it's so pretty.

Twenty minutes later, she arrived.

I will definitely get my exercise this summer.

Lacey was in high spirits.

I'm going to meet so many fun animals.

She parked in the driveway, pulled off her backpack, placed the lanyard keys holder around her neck, and donned her Crittercam hat. She opened the pet file book. This was the first time Lacey read one of Charlotte's notes in the files. One thing she recalled about Charlotte from school was that she had very sloppy handwriting. Charlotte always took short, cryptic notes in class that only Charlotte could transcribe.

The form had "DOG" checked off with "TWO" and "Gracie and Buddy" written in. The boxes, "LET OUT IN BACK YARD", "WATER", and "TREATS" were checked off. Lacey's eyes scanned down to the special file note at the bottom. Charlotte's chicken-scratch handwriting was familiar.

wild__warning_wonk

Huh?

The only word she could make out from Charlotte's sloppy handwriting was wild and warning.

Thanks, Charlotte.

There was a four-digit garage code on the form so she didn't need a key. Lacey returned the lanyard and notebook to her backpack and used the code. The door lifted to reveal a white SUV. Two bicycles were hanging on the walls. An extra refrigerator sat to the left of this spotless and organized garage. Next to the fridge sat shelves with bug spray, car wax, bleach, dry dog food, deer repellent, flashlights, bags of rags, a large bucket, and more.

Lacey tried the door that led into the house. It was unlocked.

Yip, yip, yip!

Two pet crates shook and rumbled with adorable captives. Buddy and Gracie squealed with delight.

Notice me! No! Notice me!!

Lacey identified Gracie as the older tan and white Chihuahua mix because of her pink harness. She was a little powerhouse, small, but sturdy. Her little nub tail was wagging faster than a bobblehead doll. Lacey opened the door and Gracie practically knocked her over with enthusiasm and kisses.

Giggling, Lacey said, "Hi Gracie, aren't you a happy girl? I'm Lacey."

While Gracie was finding the perfect spot on her lap, Lacey scooted over to the next crate to meet the miniature Doberman Pinscher puppy, Buddy.

He's adorable!

His black and tan markings on his little puppy face sent the convincing message, you know I'm adorable. Let me out so we can play.

Lacey opened the crate and Buddy leaped onto her and landed on top of Gracie. He didn't seem to notice or care that he was on Gracie's head. This evolved into a hysterical wrestling match between the two of them. They growled and whined with their tiny mouths wide open.

Lacey did her best deep-voiced announcer impression. "Ladies and gentlemen, welcome to Pup WrestleMania." Gracie and Buddy fell off her lap and continued grappling on the floor.

Lacey barked in her announcer's voice. "In this corner, weighing approximately fifteen pounds, we have Gracie the Chi-Chi. And in this corner, weighing in at a whopping five pounds or roughly the size of a small watermelon, we have Buddy the Min Pin."

By this point, Gracie had successfully pinned Buddy down for about eight seconds before he wriggled out from under her. They rolled over again and relocated the tournament to the nearby dog bed. Lacey was about to make another wrestling announcement when their growling and squealing rose to a whole new level. Lacey laughed at their silly show.

"You guys are like two cartoon characters. Okay, it's time to get serious about backyard duties—or should I say doodies." *Sometimes I crack myself up.*

Lacey opened the back door. "Let's go outside, you little monkeys!"

Still chasing each other, Gracie and Buddy bounded out onto the large deck and into the huge yard. Lacey strolled out onto the deck to watch Gracie and Buddy.

Easy peasy lemon squeezy.

They both ran over to the left playing, yipping, and marking their spots. Lacey noticed a movement to the right of the expansive yard. Something large was moving out of the trees.

10

STINK WARS

A huge buck with full antlers was standing in the yard eating leaves from a bushy area. Buddy and Gracie went ballistic! Like a tiny attack team, they took off running toward the large deer and barking at the top of their lungs.

Alarmed, Lacey ran down into the yard, screaming, "Gracie, Buddy, come here! Here pups! Heel! Right now!"

Her frantic shouts fell on deaf ears. Gracie and Buddy were in the battle zone. The buck backed up. He appeared to be sizing them up and thinking should I run away, attack, or fall down laughing.

It would have been funny except Lacey worried that the male deer would kick or gut one of the minuscule combatants. She grabbed Gracie by her pink harness, rescuing her from the deer zone of danger. Meanwhile, Buddy the Barbarian kept moving toward the deer who had decided that kicking was the way to go. Lacey was in a full panic. Every time she lunged for Buddy, he changed direction and slipped away. She couldn't catch the little rascal. She had to think fast. Suddenly the deer repellent flashed in her memory. It was in the garage on the shelf.

Still holding Gracie, Lacey took off running toward the garage as fast as she could. She dropped Gracie in the kitchen and ran into the garage to get the repellent. There was a bottle marked "Deer Repellent Liquid Fence". Next to it was something that looked like a flashlight, "Ultrasonic Deer Zapper".

I don't know anything about stags or repellant. I just need to rescue Buddy before he gets a fatal kick to his little Buddy-head.

She grabbed the zapper and, in her haste, knocked over the large bottle of repellent. The top broke off and liquid started to leak down the shelves onto the garage floor.

I'll clean that up later.

She ran back into the kitchen, past Gracie, and onto the back deck. She made sure to close the door on her way out.

From the deck, she could see Buddy and deer-matrix still going at it.

Buddy is relentless.

Lacey ran toward the battlefield of large buck vs. tiny buccaneer screaming "Buddy off! Heel deer! Buddy release!" Lacey turned the zapper on and pointed it at the deer.

Sorry, Mr. Deer!

Seconds later, the buck took off toward the rear fence. Without looking back, he leaped over the hurdle in one jump. Lacey's heart was pounding. She ran over to examine him for any injuries. The Min Pin pup was no worse for wear.

Buddy was still wound up and barking, his tiny body begging, let me at him! I can take him! Lacey scooped him up. "I can't decide whether to spank you or hug you". She held Buddy close to her. "Buddy, you scared the scare out of me." She carried him back into the house.

That's when the smell hit her. A pungent odor was oozing into the kitchen through the closed garage door. It smelled like a million rotten eggs baking in the hot sun. Lacey ran into the garage and almost fell over. The stench was overwhelming. The deer repellent had run all the way down the shelf and was puddling on the cement floor.

Lacey almost gagged. "Ruh-roh! That's disgusting!"

She grabbed a rag and held it over her mouth.

What a nightmare! I have to clean this up.

While Gracie and Buddy slept in the kitchen, Lacey scrubbed the floors in the garage. Finally, after an hour, the million rotten eggs lessened to a hundred rotten eggs.

Yuck!

Almost two hours after she arrived at her first job, bright-eyed and bushy-tailed, an exhausted and smelly Lacey took her camera hat off, put it in the backpack, and got on her bike to go to job number two. Am I going to make it there in time?

11

MUNCHKIN WHISPERS

Lacey didn't have time to go home and shower. As she pedaled like a crazy person to the next appointment, she smelled like Pig Pen from the Peanuts comic strip. She could visualize a black stink cloud encircling her. Lacey was sure that her body odor arrived at the next house ten minutes before she did. Each time the breeze switched in her direction, she gagged.

Forget deer repellent, this stuff could repel dinosaurs—purchase now and we'll send you two cans of Dino-repel for the price of one!

She arrived at the townhouse marked on the map with an "X". It was a small street with connected homes in groups of four. No one was around when she parked her bike in the driveway. She put on her pink hat and opened the notebook to read the file. The boxes checked off under instructions were, "CAT", "FEED", "WATER", and "SCOOP LITTER".

The cat's name is Munchkin, how cute!

Lacey glared at Charlotte's top-secret, super important file note.

wag_swe_t.

She stared at the messy marks masquerading as vital information. "Seriously Charlotte?" Her handwriting was so unreadable, it was top secret to everyone. Too bad Charlotte didn't include a spy decoder pen in her backpack.

Lacey used the code to unlock the door and went inside the townhouse. As soon as she closed the door, she saw a tan cat with extremely short legs hopping down the stairs.

I've read about this rare breed of cats. The dwarf cat is specially bred to have short little legs. Munchkin is a compact cube of cuteness.

She bounced down the stairs to greet Lacey. Then the weirdest thing happened. Just as she was about to rub on Lacey's legs, her fur stood at attention. Munchkin lifted her cherub face in the air. Her nose and whiskers quivered furiously.

Munchkin's stumpy legs launched her straight up and she let out a "YOWL!" Her nose was convulsing as she landed and slowly backed away from Lacey.

Poor Munchkin is repelled by the deer repellent! Kitty no-likey stinky.

Lacey had to think fast. She didn't want to frighten Munchkin with her audacious odor. She mentally scanned the training bookshelf in her room and remembered the book "From Lions into Kittens". According to the book, Lacey must camouflage offensive smells the way lions do in the wild.

How can I disguise the deer repellent with a smell more tempting to Munchkin's sensitive snout?

The offended kitty had now flipped over on her back and was furiously rubbing her eyes with both paws. Lacey had a light bulb moment. She retrieved the wet cat food packet from her Charlotte's Critters bag and stuck her fingers inside. She patted the mushy "Duck Lover's Delight" on her neck and wrists, just like her mother did with perfume.

Duck Lover's Perfume, coming soon to a fine perfumery near you.

Lacey thought *yuck!*

Munchkin thought duck!

Lacey seized the opportunity to win her over. She settled flat on the floor, she looked directly into Munchkin's eyes and slowly opened and closed her eyes three times.

Cats can't resist this move.

The sweet-eyes technique is a way to get the cat to mirror you. Lacey slowly opened and closed her eyes two more times.

Wait for it. Wait for it.

Blink.

Yes! Ladies and gentlemen, Lacey still has it! Reeking of rotten eggs and Duck Lover's Delight—not to mention deadly body odor, Lacey Honeycut is THE CAT WHISPERER!

Munchkin gave a sweet "meeah-ah" and stood up. At least it looked like she was standing; it was hard to tell with those stumpy little legs. She strutted over to Lacey and nuzzled her nose.

"Hi Munchkin, I'm so sorry for smelling like rotten eggs. Do you like my new cologne better?"

Munchkin purred and nuzzled her nose into Lacey's outstretched hands. Each time she flipped around; her cute little tail wagged like a puppy dog.

"Now I understand Charlotte's file note. You wag your tail just like a puppy dog and you are sweet."

Lacey played with Munchkin for a little while, mostly rubbing her belly. Munchkin followed Lacey up the stairs, into the kitchen. She gave her fresh water, filled her dry food, and opened a new Kitty Morsels package. Munchkin's food bowl had a surprise! A small felt mouse sat in the bowl as a hint to the staff—feed me!

"Move over mousey, it's feeding time."

Lacey moved the toy mouse and squeezed the wet food out. Munchkin pushed her head in the bowl before Lacey finished squeezing.

Lacey laughed. "Hey! You might be eating my perfume!"

Munchkin followed her downstairs to scoop out the litter box and watched Lacey through the glass door as she watered the potted flowers on the deck. Lacey filled out the pet sitting report card then rubbed Munchkin's fluffy head.

"Bye Munchkin kitty. See you soon!"

Outside, Lacey entered the code to lock the door. She was about to take off her camera cap when wet sailor Wigglesworth appeared.

12

STINKY INTERROGATION

Wilma Wigglesworth wore a black two-piece business suit with a white carnation in her lapel and a chunky pearl necklace. She whipped out a small pen and notebook. On the front cover, it said, "Society for Women of the Volunteer Neighborhood Watch Committee." On the back, "Wilma W. Wigglesworth, Volunteering Volunteer."

She launched right into an interrogation. "Young lady, state your name and purpose for loitering on my neighbor's private property."

Holding up the pink backpack that read "Charlotte's Critters,", Lacey said, "I'm Lacey Honeycut. I'm helping my friend Charlotte with her pet-sitting and dog-walking business while she's in Wales."

She demanded, "State your full name, address, phone number, social security number, parents' full names, number of siblings and pets in your household, driver's license, automobile registration and tag number."

She paused and looked at Lacey again. "Scratch those last three items. I'll also need the name of the person who gave you written permission for standing on this private property."

Lacey stared at Mrs. Wigglesworth.

Mrs. Wigglesworth stared at Lacey.

It was at that precise moment that the wind picked up and a gust blew directly from Lacey into Mrs. Wigglesworth's face. The combination of deer repellent and cat food—cat-apellent—proved too much for the Director of the Current Inquisition. Making a face that Lacey could only describe as pukeadelic, Mrs. Wigglesworth quickly pinched her nose shut with one hand. Her face colored to the perfect shade of pea green soup. She looked at the Charlotte's Critters backpack. Then she looked at Lacey's smeared cat food neck.

In a shaky, high nasal voice she announced, "Young lady, it is my duty to inform you that heretofore I am filing a formal complaint with the Society of Women for Clean and Cleaner Air for the Prevention of Hazmat Threats." She verified with her gold wristwatch and added, "The time is two forty-five p.m."

Lacey was dumbfounded. Dumb meaning unable to speak and founded referring to couldn't found or find her voice.

Mrs. Wigglesworth snapped the tiny notebook shut. She spun on her high heels and almost tripped. As she retreated, she shouted, "Lacey Honeycut, you have been verbally cited and warned by a volunteer member of the Society for Women of the Volunteer Neighborhood Watch."

Lacey watched Mrs. Wigglesworth disappear around the corner.

I'm in big trouble.

13

WIGGLES WORLD

On her walk home, Mrs. Wigglesworth mumbled to herself. She often mumbled to herself when she was agitated. Mrs. Wigglesworth was highly agitated.

"Charlotte's Critters—*MY BOTTOM!* I've never liked varmints! I only tell people I'm allergic to darling little pets so I don't have to have any interaction with the distasteful buggers. They stink and leave fur everywhere. They don't clean up after themselves. They don't pay taxes or register to vote. They don't carry health insurance. They have sharp teeth and claws and they can't be trusted! I need to report this incident as soon as possible!"

She arrived home. Even in her haste to save the town's breathable air, she couldn't help but stop and admire her house. A white sign above the door read "Turkey Hill Tribute House". The white two-story farmhouse-style-home was her pride and joy. She had the custom Turkey Hill home built as a replica of Martha Stewart's first house. Mrs. Wigglesworth idolized Martha Helen Stewart and everything "Martha Stewart Living".

The first thing she did when she got inside was to remove her painful high heels. She wiped each one off with a shoe towel and placed them carefully on the shoe rack in the hall closet. In the kitchen, she stood in front of her Amazon Echo Show.

"Alexa, call the Society of Women for Clean and Cleaner Air for the Prevention of Hazmat Threats."

Alexa replied, "Calling the Society of Women for Mean and Meaner Bears for the Prevention of Threats."

Mrs. Wigglesworth repeated, "Mean Bears? No!"

In a stern voice, she said, "Alexa. Cancel."

Alexa replied, "Canceling."

Mrs. Wigglesworth tried again, this time enunciating her words slowly and carefully as if speaking to a small child.

"Alexa, call the SOCIETY OF WOMEN FOR CLEAN AND CLEANER AIR FOR THE PREVENTION OF HAZMAT THREATS."

In her smooth robotic voice, Alexa replied, "Calling the Society for Green and Greener Pears for the Prevention of Sweat."

Mrs. Wigglesworth lost it. She shouted, "Alexa, cancel! You're an idiot!"

In her polite voice, Alexa replied, "Cancelling. I'm sorry you feel that way."

Mrs. Wigglesworth turned Alexa off. "Do I have to do everything myself?"

She took out her cell phone and googled the hotline number. She heard two rings and then an automated voice said, "You've reached the reporting hotline for the Society of Women for Clean and Cleaner Air for the Prevention of Hazmat Threats. We are currently dealing with urgent matters to keep your air safe. At the sound of the tone, please leave a detailed message. A member of our team will respond in a timely manner."

An answering machine? What kind of a hotline was this?

Mrs. Wigglesworth heard a long beep. She had no choice. She left a message in her most impressive Power-Woman-Take-Charge voice. "This is Mrs. Wilma Wren. Wigglesworth. I am filing a verbal incident report on behalf of the Society for Women of the Volunteer Neighborhood Watch, of which I am a volunteer. In fact, some would consider me the head volunteer. Please call me back at your earliest convenience regarding an urgent hazmat incident that I personally witnessed in my neighborhood in Meriwether Pines. It involves a troublemaker named Lacey Honeycut."

She left her cell phone number, address, Martha Stewart Fan Club identification number, social security number, email address, and home number before hanging up. She made a cup of hibiscus-mint iced tea, a Martha Stewart recipe, and sat in her Martha Stewart rocking chair. A few sips of the tea calmed her nerves.

On the table next to her rocking chair sat a framed photograph of her late mother, Wahnita Wren Wigglesworth, or WWII as she was affectionately called. She and her mother looked so much alike. She had her same hawkish, pointed nose, closely set small brown eyes, and a strong chin. It was what her mother called her Power Chin. Mother Wahnita always said, "A powerful chin for a powerful woman."

Mrs. Wigglesworth came from a long line of Power Women. Her mother, grandmother, and great-grandmother were all past women's society presidents. Ever since her husband passed away ten years ago, Mrs. Wigglesworth made it her life's focus to become as well respected as they had been. She still had not achieved her goal as the president of a women's society, other than the one she created. She had joined so many prestigious women's societies, but alas, no titles.

It was important to be important. Today she filed the report because she had to. It was her social responsibility—wasn't it? Taking another sip of hibiscus-mint tea, she set her strong chin tight and remembered the constant childhood scolding from Mother Wahnita. "Wilma, NOBODY likes a tattletale!"

The manager at the Society of Women for Clean and Cleaner Air for the Prevention of Hazmat Threats checked the hotline messages. Alarmed by what she heard; she immediately filed a report. Her report generated a Red Flag Report.

Hours later, a Red Flag Report marked 'CONFIDENTIAL' was sent via text to a top-secret cell phone. A tall, skinny man and a short, robust man read the text together.

The tall man stroked his bushy mustache deep in thought.

The short man stroked his bushy mustache deep in thought.

Tall man said, "Looks like they're putting us on this case because we're already here in Meriwether Pines."

Shorter man said, "We've been riding around on this golf cart for two days, using the best technical surveillance equipment that money can buy and we haven't found any illegal money counterfeiting houses. Now we're supposed to handle an air pollution report?"

Tall and skinny said, "We're FBI agents. The government

has to justify our expenses while staying in this small town. Remember, we're acting on a solid lead that criminals are renting houses in small towns to make fake money and then moving the new money out through the local banks."

"Do you think this Wigglesworth hazardous air pollution report is connected?"

14

STINKY SAD

Lacey arrived home just as her family was sitting down for dinner. The putrid scent of Lacey's unique catapellent quickly overpowered the aroma of Mom's cooking. Mom dropped her fork. "What is that awful stench?"

Petey wrinkled his little nose and started crying. Steve looked over at Lacey, still planted near the doorway and said, "That stank reminds me of my dad."

Mom raised her eyebrows and looked at Steve.

He shook his head back and forth, laughing. "No, sorry, I didn't mean he smelled like that. He hated deer coming on our property and used a lot of deer repellent. Lacey, have you been on some kind of anti-hunting protest?"

Planted in the doorway, afraid to come closer to anyone, she looked down and mumbled, "No, not an activist day."

Mom admonished her. "Whatever it is, go directly into the laundry room, strip down, and put everything you are wearing, and I mean everything, directly into the washing machine. Put extra detergent in and wash everything in hot water with an extra rinse. Then wrap yourself in a towel and go directly to your bathroom. Understood?"

"Understood."

As Mom was comforting poor Petey, she shouted, "Scrub from head to toe! Head to toe! Then come back down for dinner and tell us why you stink."

Lacey stomped up the stairs feeling down in the dumps. She was a girl who always tried so hard to do the right thing. Today had been a total disaster. Charlotte was counting on her. Lacey never got in trouble and now this bizarre Wigglesworth woman was trying to get her in trouble, BIG TROUBLE. She was actually going to report Lacey to some kind of regulatory organization.

I have to figure out what to do. I never hide things from Mom but I can't tell her about this.

When she stepped into her room, she saw Drowsy and Mickey napping together with her Scooby-Doo doll. Their little noses began to quiver. Their eyes flew open wide. They looked at her then looked at each other. Without a meow or a squeak, they both leaped from the bed and ran past her out the door.

Traitors. Good to know I can count on my animals when the going gets tough.

Lacey stood in the hot shower. A single tear ran down her cheek.

All I want to do is help a friend and take care of some animals.

Lacey wasn't a girl who cried. Ever since her parents got divorced, and before Steve came along, Lacey felt that she had to be strong and grown-up to be there for her mom. She saw herself as a girl who liked to always focus on the positive. She was the rescuer. She was the one who always made her friends laugh and lifted them up. And now she needed some encouragement.

Once Lacey was dressed and smelled like a human being again, she sat at her desk and plugged her walky into the charger. She wasn't ready to go downstairs and face her family yet. She noticed a postcard sitting on the desk next to the charger and picked it up. On one side was a stunning photo of a beautiful castle. "Cardiff, Wales" was written below it. On the back, the postcard was addressed to her and postmarked. It must have arrived that day.

Mom probably put it on my desk.

In actual legible handwriting, Charlotte wrote, "Dear Lacey, my uncle insists that I send postcards this summer to improve my 'atrocious handwriting'. Wales is beautiful. It's so green here. Miss you all. By the way, make sure to always walk Buddy and Gracie on a leash to avoid the wildlife."

Lacey sad face turned to giggles. *Seriously?* Charlotte's postcard cracked her up. It was just the silly bit of sunshine she needed. Charlotte's timing with explaining her file notes may be horribly off, but her timing to cheer up Lacey was spot on.

This just in, Charlotte's timing is so bad, she thinks a timetable is a table you place clocks on.

The walky in front of her started squawking. "Walky-talky #2, this is walky-talky #1, come in, over."

15

SKYPE DANCING

Lacey grabbed her walky and said, "Walky #2, I'm here. Go ahead, over."

Maxwell said, "Hi Lacey. How was your first day? Over."

Lacey muttered into the speaker, "Let's just say highly memorable. There's so much to tell you and no way that I can explain it all on the walkies. I'm headed downstairs for dinner. Can you rendezvous with Anna and schedule an eight p.m. Skype meeting with Team Critter tonight? Over."

"Will do. Team Critter meeting, Skype eight p.m. Over and out."

By the time Lacey got back to the dinner table, dinner was over. Her plate was covered with tinfoil and waiting for her. She could hear Mom on the baby monitor giving Petey a bath. He loved bath time.

Lacey uncovered her plate and dug into it. She was starving and also relieved not to have to answer any questions about today. It had been a rough start to the summer. She finished her dinner, downed her glass of milk, and loaded her dishes in the dishwasher.

She went into Steve's office and logged onto Skype with her password. Maxwell and Anna were already there.

Friends, I feel better already.

She smiled and waved. "Hi guys, I'm so happy to see you both. You will not believe what happened today!"

Lacey launched into a detailed description of her day. She talked and talked and talked. Maxwell and Anna sat there in front of their Skype screens speechless and completely mesmerized by her story. She told them about her encounter with Wilma Wigglesworth. When Lacey was finished describing her day, she was exhausted and relieved. She ended the story, saying, "Day one, insane, check that box."

Maxwell leaned into his computer screen and said, "What a wild ride!"

Anna said, "I told you that lady was daffy as a duck."

Maxwell asked, "What was the name of the organization that she was going to file a report with? I can research it for you."

Lacey said, "Honestly, I don't remember. I was so shocked at the time, that it's all one big blur. There's no way I can tell my parents. They would want to take over my Charlotte's Critters duties for the rest of the summer and I would look like a complete flunkey when Charlotte got back."

Maxwell said, "Did you still have your Crittercam hat on when she was talking to you?"

"Yes."

"Good, I'll download the video and get the name of the organization."

Anna said, "I'd like to see that video just to see Daffy Duck in action."

Maxwell said, "I'll research it for you, but don't sweat it, I'm sure she's just a nosey neighbor who doesn't like kids.

Swallowing hard, Lacey said, "Okay, thanks, Maxwell."

Anna said, "Lacey, I know that you're tired and you feel like you bombed but I've got just what you need. Maxwell, are you up for a spontaneous rapcheer?"

Lacey slapped her hand on her forehead and said, "Oh no, not a rapcheer."

Maxwell stood up and pulled his chair back. He pointed the camera up so it could get a full-body shot of him in the Skype session. Maxwell may be a brilliant geek, but he had skills. The boy could dance hip hop and break-dance! He was on a hip-hop dance team.

Maxwell struck a pose and started the *rat-ta-tat-ta-tat-ta-tat* then the *pe-petu-pe-petu-pe-petu*.

Anna jumped right in with a spontaneous rhyme.

"Lacey don't fret, it ain't over yet, with Charlotte's pets.

They can't be hoodwinked by that super stink, they're still tickled pink.

Deer chase dogs, cats love bullfrogs; soon you'll be writing your own pet blog

Forgive my lame rhyme and his pantomime; we didn't have any advance prep time."

Maxwell added a few more sound effects and ended with a hip-hop slide back into his chair—almost toppling over.

Lacey was laughing and applauding. The performance lifted her spirits. She stood up still clapping, "Bravo! Bravo! A standing ovation for the rapcheer duo!"

That night, Lacey fell asleep as soon as her head hit the pillow. Her last thought was, *is this woman going to make Charlotte lose her business? Will I get blamed?*

16

LACEY'S ROOM

When she woke up, she could hear the rain hitting the window. It was going to be a muddy day at the stables. Drowsy was stretched out across Lacey, purring and Mickey was curled up on Lacey's extra pillow. Lacey looked over at the clock and realized she had slept in. It was already 9:45 a.m.

Yesterday's drama and the soothing rain had created the perfect storm for snoozeville. She felt rested.

Today is a new day.

Lacey stretched her arms up high and gave one huge yawn. She leaned over and kissed Drowsy on top of her head and scratched Mickey's back. "Good morning sleepyheads."

Lacey's bedroom was decorated in her favorite color. She had a white queen-size sleigh bed. Her bedspread and throw pillows were lavender with yellow dragonflies. More throw pillows were scattered on the bed and the floor near a bean bag chair. A white hand-painted desk faced the large window, draped with lavender and white polka-dotted curtains.

Three framed posters of Scooby-Doo hung on her wall. Lacey was obsessed with Scooby-Doo and his gang. The first poster was Scooby-Doo, Shaggy, Velma, Fred, and Daphne all grouped together in front of the Mystery Machine Van. In this poster, they were clearly in the middle of mystery-solving-madness. The second poster was for the *Zombie Island* movie and the third was from Hanna Barbera Studios. It showed Velma crawling on the ground trying to find her glasses while a large Frankenstein-type monster leered over her with Scooby and Shaggy freaking out. This was Lacey's favorite and a gift from her dad.

On Lacey's desk were several framed photos. The largest was of Sir Lancelot. Anna took this photo when she was helping Lacey at Huntclub. In the picture, Lancelot was in his stall. It was a close-up of his horsey face and he looked like he was smiling. Next to that was a framed photo collage of Drowsy and Mickey in various poses. In one picture, the blue mouse slept on top of Drowsy's head—both cat and mouse seemed unaware that they should be arch enemies.

Lacey never understood their relationship. The day she brought Mickey home and placed him in front of Drowsy, she expected them to go after each other and was prepared to play referee. Then the weirdest thing happened. Drowsy crouched down ready to pounce and cocked her head in confusion. A few minutes later, Drowsy stood up, stretched and yawned then walked over to her bed for a nap. Ever since then, they had been fast friends.

The last framed photo was a close-up of four-year-old Lacey sticking her tongue out at the camera. Her wild, light brown hair stood up with static cling. This photo cracked Lacey up. Mom took the picture. Lacey remembered what Mom said right before she snapped the picture. "Lacey, you're not a grown-up yet." That's when Lacey stuck her tongue out at the camera—and at Mom.

Mom doted on her at times but mostly encouraged her daughter's independence. As long as they had trust, they were good. That's why Lacey didn't like keeping this Wigglesworth secret from Mom.

I'll fix everything, then mom won't need to know.

The largest wall in her room was lined with bookshelves from floor to ceiling. Lacey referred to this as the Wall of Knowledge. Since the age of four, Lacey had been collecting books, magazines, and movies as part of a plan to become an expert in each category. A sign at the top of each bookshelf identified the theme. A mini-shelf was first with all things Scooby-Doo: movies, books, DVDs, and more. Lacey loved borrowing the mystery gang's sayings: Zoinks, Rooby-Roo, Ruh-Roh, Jeepers, Groovy, Jinkies, and more.

Bookshelf one was labeled "Whispering".

Some of her favorite books were"

Animal Whisperers of Ancient Times,

Dog Whispering—Fact or Fiction,

A Whisper in the Dark: Advantages of animal training without light,

How to Unwhisper Bad Behavior in Your Pet,

An Interplanetary Guide to Alien Animal Whispering,

and *Whispering in Foreign Languages.*

Movies and DVDs included Cesar Millan's *Dog Whisperer* and *The Horse Whisperer.*

Lacey was fascinated by mammals, birds, reptiles, and amphibians. She considered herself an expert in their behaviors. If it slithered, hopped, flew, or walked, she studied it.

The next bookshelf was "Training". Top book pics were"

Litter Quitter: Train your cat to use the toilet in 48 hours,

Talk to Me: How I taught my deaf parrot to speak,

Hollywood's Top Animal Trainers,
Giraffes: Are they too tall to train?,
and *True Training Confessions from a Circus Performer.*

DVDs and movies contained *Lassie* (the complete series), *Marley & Me*, *Doctor Dolittle*, and the complete series of *My Cat from Hell*.

The third bookshelf was labeled, "Veterinarian and Inventor Lacey Honeycut". Lacey was working on filling this one.

Lacey changed into her faded blue jeans and a gray t-shirt. The shirt had a picture of a girl wearing Wellington boots in a muddy horse field. It read "Forget glass slippers, this princess wears boots." Her dad gave her this shirt for her birthday last year. She loved it so much that it was faded from constant wash and wear.

She ran a brush through her light brown hair and pulled it into a ponytail. Her horse-riding boots were downstairs in the garage. She always put them on when she left. They were "under no circumstances allowed in the house".

In the kitchen chocolate-covered brother Petey sat in his high chair holding the last chunk of a cookie. He flashed Lacey a chocolate-chip smile. "Wacey!"

Lacey tousled his dark hair. "How's my baby bro today?"

Mom wiped Petey's sticky hands and face with a washcloth. "You're just in time for cold chocolate chip pancakes. Do you want some milk with that?"

Lacey said, "Yes, please Mom, I'm starving."

Petey was in his high chair making a huge mess with what was left of his breakfast. He was wearing more food on his face than what was left on the plate. This seemed to delight him even more. He was laughing and clapping. Every time he clapped; food would go flying to the floor from his sticky hands.

Lacey loved her little brother. He was the cutest kid.

Mom asked "Did you get the postcard from Charlotte on your desk?"

"Yup."

"That was nice of her to think of you. I'm taking Petey to the mall with me to do some shopping. Do you want to go with us this morning?"

"Thanks, but I'm going to go spend some time with Lancelot. He needs a good brushing and some attention."

Lacey put her dishes in the sink and grabbed a juice box from the refrigerator.

Mom said. "Lacey, dishes in the dishwasher."

Lacey sighed. "Okay, Mom.".

Mom shook her head. "My daughter, who can't help clean in the house is the same child who pedals madly off in the pouring rain to spend hours feeding a horse and mucking out its stable."

Lacey spent the rest of the morning with Lancelot in his stall. She brushed him all over and combed out his long tail. He was a beautiful horse. He was still a little bit too big for her, but when she grew taller, he would be just right. She scraped his hooves then pulled out the hose. "Here's your favorite part, boy," she said to him. He loved getting rinsed off.

When they were alone in his stall like this, Lacey sang to him or just cooed in her best horsey baby-talk voice. "You're such a handsome beast, Sir Lancelot. One day you're going to be mine, all mine". Lacey gave him a firm pat on the rump and said, "See you later, horsey face. I got some cats who are just dying to meet me."

Lacey parked her bicycle up in front of the large two-story house, took her backpack off and opened the file. The 'CAT' box was checked off with 'TWO, BLACK' next to it. 'FOOD',

'WATER', and 'TREATS' were also checked. The owner wrote the pets' names as Dr. Evil and Shadow.

DR. EVIL? The cat is named DR. EVIL?

17

EVIL SHADOW

Seriously?

She put on her hat and pulled out the key chain. Lacey looked at the special file note made by Charlotte.

Here we go again.

D_evilo__nosc-op.

Lacey squeezed her eyes tight then opened them and stared at the words, hoping to hypnotize them into making sense. No luck. The only part understandable was the beginning—most likely Dr. Evil.

Okay Charlotte, you wanted to tell me something vitally important about Dr. Evil.

She burst into giggles at the absurdity of the cryptic note. What else could she do? It was as if Charlotte was from the planet Mars and Lacey didn't speak Martian. Lacey announced out loud, "Ready or not, here I come!"

Exactly 31 things happened next.

1.Lacey unlocked the door and stepped inside.

2.A large black cat appeared out of nowhere and blocked her passageway.

3. Lacey slammed the door shut to prevent the cat's escape.

4. At the sound of the door slam, a smaller black cat bounded up the stairs.

5. The first black cat performed a ninja flyby, clawing Lacey's shoulder on the way.

6. Lacey screamed out, "Ouchy! Magouchy!"

7. The big black cat landed above her head on a cabinet.

8. Sensing danger, Lacey ran toward the kitchen, covering her head.

9. Somehow the bionic supercat landed on the kitchen counter directly in front of her.

10. Lacey spied a laundry room to her left.

11. Lacey made an instant decision.

12. Lacey dashed toward the laundry room and ran inside.

13. Lacey hid behind the door next to a cat litter box.

14. The cat litter box began making a motor noise and scooping litter.

15. The silent warrior cat materialized on top of the washing machine.

16. Lacey ran out and kicked the door closed.

17. Lacey stood in front of the laundry room to catch her breath.

18. The words get in and get out alive, ran through her mind.

19. Lacey pictured the checklist.

20. "Litterbox" (self-scooping). Check!

21. "Water bowl". Lacey grabbed the bowl from the floor and filled it. Check!

22. "Food". Lacey grabbed the food bag and poured it into the feeder. Check!

23. "Treats". Forget about it! Or not?

24. Lacey grabbed the bag of treats and emptied it in front of

the laundry room door.

25. Lacey exclaimed, "On your mark, get set, catapult!"

26. Lacey opened the laundry room door.

27. Dr. Evil (clearly his name) materialized, hissing, and howling at her.

28. Lacey's heart skipped exactly FIVE beats.

29. Dr. Evil spied the treats and began to devour them.

30. Lacey sprinted toward the front door.

31. Lacey exited the house of horrors.

Lacey re-locked the front door and sat down on the stoop to catch her breath. Her heart was beating so fast she could feel it in her throat.

I've never been attacked by a cat before or any animal. I've also never met a cat named Dr. Evil. Is this some kind of Charlotte's Critters curse? I'm great with animals. I'm fantastic with cats. Heck, I live and sleep with a cat. I am the female Dr. Dolittle. This cat-uation slid downhill so quickly that I didn't have time to be a cat whisperer.

She inspected the small cuts on her shoulder.

"Oucheehuhua! Ouch! Ouch!"

The scratches were small, but they stung like a group of yellow jacket bees were playing Red Rover and asked her shoulders to come over.

"Oucheehuhua!"

Somehow shouting eased the pain and recharged Lacey. A wave of defiance hit her. Who did that evil villain think he was? She turned towards the door and hollered, "You're a mangy black furball with a bad attitude!"

That's it, this is war! I have to visit Dr. Evil and Shadow again because the owners are out of town. It's time to call in the troops.

She pulled out her walky-talky. "Maxwell! Anna! Come in!

Mayday! Cat attack, a complete *cat-tastrophy*! Over."

Maxwell pushed the red button. "Walky #2. This is walky #1. Lacey, I'm here. What's going on? Where are you? Are you okay? Over."

Lacey recapped her mauled and mugged mews to Maxwell. She ended the story with, "That's why I think Dr. Evil is possessed! Here's the worst part. I have to go back there again tomorrow. Charlotte's Critters is responsible for taking care of friendly and fiendish felines. I took THE VOW! I have to face that crazy, attack zombie cat one more time."

Maxwell let out a long whistle over the walky. "Ten-four loud and clear, Feline Zombie Apocalypse. Over."

Regardless of her predicament, Feline Zombie Apocalypse made Lacey laugh. She sat on the front steps and examined her war wounds.

Note to self, add Band-Aids and disinfectant to knapsack.

She said, "Walky #2, Maxwell, thanks for making me laugh. I needed that. You're the big ideas guy. Any lightbulb ideas on how I can complete this duty of danger all in one piece? Over."

Maxwell said, "Walky #2, Lacey, give me a minute to wrap my brain-pan around this. Over." After a few minutes of radio silence, Maxwell broadcast on the walky. "This is walky #1. Lacey, you have requested assistance with a hooligan housecat. After a few minutes of brainstorming, I am convinced that I've got the dilemma debunked. Over."

Lacey breathed a sigh of relief. Maxwell was quirky but oh so clever. She had complete faith in him. She said, "Walky #1, this is walky #2. Knock me out with your diabolical plan! Over."

Just then, Anna's alarmed voice interrupted. "Walkies—I mean walky team, are you okay? Is anyone hurt? Hello? Was it Wigglesworth again? Damage control, can you hear me?

Anyone?"

Maxwell responded, "Walky #3, please remember your training and protocol!"

Anna replied, "Roger that, walky #1 and #2. Sorry! I heard cat-tastrophy and freaked out! I was helping my mom at the salon with a perm. Man, that stuff stinks! I had to wait and step outside."

Maxwell said, "That's okay, team member. I know this is a new modus operandi for you. My dad has hammered into me you need to be extra calm during duress and always converse using designated terms. That's the only way a detective can do his job."

Anna said, "Okeydokey. I have no experience with this type of mission. Actually—any type of mission." She started giggling and added, "Over."

Lacey piped in before Maxwell could reprimand poor Anna about giggling. Maxwell took this handheld radio jargon so seriously. She spoke into her walky in a language she knew Anna would relate to—rhyming. "Walky #3, thanks for your call and being on the ball. Maxwell has it all under wraps. No more cat traps. We'll report back to you when the cat-tastrophy is through. Over."

Maxwell said, "Walkies #2 and #3, thank you for your response. I'll meet Lacey at the cat combatant's house tomorrow to execute my plan. By the way, I reviewed the Crittercam video and got the name of the organization that Wigglesworth reported you to. It's the Society of Women for Clean and Cleaner Air for the Prevention of Hazmat Threats. It's some kind of governmental agency."

Lacey heard governmental and almost dropped her walky. She said, "Walky #1, should I be worried? Out."

18

EVIL SOLUTIONS

Maxwell reassured her, "I wouldn't worry if I were you. You smelled like my dirty socks but you weren't polluting the air. The entire thing makes zero sense to me. I'll let you know if I find out anything else. Over and out."

The next morning, Lacey was wondering what Maxwell had come up with for her visit with Dr. Evil and Shadow today. Her cat Drowsy had never scratched her, but she knew that some cats were super moody. Dr. Evil left his mark yesterday. She had to admit that she was kind of scared of him, or at least nervous about another faceoff.

Lacey took commitment seriously, especially when it came to animals. They were so cute and so helpless—well, most of them were. They depended completely on humans, even the grouchy or mean ones.

I am responsible for feeding Dr. Evil and Shadow while their owners are gone. I took the Oath and I must honor it. With Maxwell's help, I will outsmart Dr. Evil!

Lacey pedaled to Dr. Evil's house. Maxwell was just pulling

up on his bicycle. He had a baby trailer hooked up to the back of his bicycle.

"Where did you get that?" she asked. "I hope you don't think I'm going to ride in it? Is that your solution?"

"No, silly. My friend Luke let me borrow it for today."

"That's a relief. I can just see the news report, 'Girl reduced to a helpless baby by a bully cat, rides home in baby trailer.'"

"Have a little faith. It's not for you to ride in. I needed some way to transport this stuff that I brought."

Maxwell unzipped the back of the trailer and pulled out a bicycle helmet with a camera mounted on it, a khaki kid's winter trench coat, a swimming mask and snorkel, long yellow rubber gloves, and a whistle on a chain.

Lacey looked at the mishmash of paraphernalia. It wasn't a pretty sight. "You're kidding, right? This is your genius solution?"

Maxwell held up the bicycle helmet, swim mask, and snorkel. He said, "Hey, I spent all morning getting this stuff together. It took me time to find the right sizes for you. I had to make my neighbor Harry try on three different sizes.

Lacey rolled her eyes and said, "It just keeps getting better. Harry was my model."

Maxwell ignored her question. "With this helmet and this mask, your face is protected. You don't want evil kitty's sharp claws to get you in the face or worse yet, claw out an eyeball! You will need the snorkel to breathe."

"Maxwell, you make an excellent case. I am pretty fond of having eyeballs."

"Since you can't wear your pink cap under or over the helmet, I rigged Anna's action camera to the top of this helmet in place of the Crittercam."

"Great Maxwell. So, you're saying this will be the sequel movie. The return of Dr. Evil."

"Not a bad idea. You'd probably get a lot of crazy cat followers on YouTube."

Lacey stuck her tongue out at Maxwell.

"As I was saying. This trench coat completely covers you all the way down to the top of your riding boots. The long yellow rubber work gloves will protect your hands. It's a completely radical, yet practical protective layer of armor."

Lacey raised her eyebrows and stared at the gear. "What's the whistle for?"

"That's a failsafe."

Lacey held up the whistle and tested it.

FWEEEEEEEEE FWEEEEE

Her ears were ringing. She asked, "What's a failsafe?"

"Use it if everything else fails, so you'll be safe."

"Clarification please."

Maxwell handed her the gear to put on. "If Dr. Evil isn't spoofed by your weird disguise and he tries to pull some naughty ninja move on you, blow the whistle as loud as you can. Animals are hypersensitive to sound. It's basically a safety net for you."

Lacey couldn't argue with Maxwell. It was a good solution. Yes, she would look ridiculous, but at least she could get the job done safely. "Okay, let's get this over with and hope no one sees me in this crazy outfit."

When Lacey was all dressed in her bizarre Princess Cat-Warrior protective gear, she was a sight to see. She could barely move with all the layers of clothes. The swim mask made it hard to see to her right and left. She put the whistle around her neck and took a deep breath through the snorkel.

FWEEEEEEEEE FWEEEEE

"Ready or not, here I come. I am a brave Warrior Princess who loves and respects animals—even the evil ones. No harm shall come to me." Then she waddled up to the front door, unlocked it, and pushed it open.

Dr. Evil was once again sitting directly inside the doorway. She quickly closed the door behind her so he couldn't get out and turned to face the black scallywag. She stared at the evildoer through the swim mask. His yellow eyes pierced right through her. The shy cat named Shadow was sitting in the living room. Shadow took one look at Lacey's armor and darted to the top of the stairs. One down, two survivors left. It was just her and Dr. Evil Eyes.

He tilted his head to the side, trying to determine if she was some kind of alien or space astronaut. Would he stand his ground? Would he try to swat at her again with his sharp kitty claws? Would he attack her face and try to claw out her eyeballs as Maxwell had warned?

I need to get this over with!

She was already sweating like crazy under all the layers of clothes, and her mask was fogging up, making it difficult to see. She tentatively stepped around the black cat to head for the kitchen.

Before Lacey's second step touched the floor, evil kitty took off like a rocket. He turned and ran, breaking all world cat speed records. He ran past Shadow and out of sight. Lacey gave a small chuckle.

Maxwell, you really are a genius.

Even though Dr. Evil was out of sight, Lacey kept the gear on until she was back outside. She wasn't in the clear yet. Lacey changed the water bowls and refilled the food dispensers. She almost spilled the second water bowl because the long rubber gloves were way too big for her. The fingers were extremely long and kept bending when she tried to pick up the bowl. The insides of both gloves were slippery because she was sweating so much!

Yuck! Even Scooby and the gang never went through this when solving a mystery! I sure hope Charlotte appreciates everything I'm doing for her.

As Lacey opened the front door to leave, she looked back to see if the creepy cat had reappeared. Through her foggy mask, she spied him sitting at the top of the staircase, gazing down at her. There was a look on his solid black kitty face of complete bewilderment. Dazed and confused, was the thought that came to mind. Lacey gave him a wave with her floppy rubber-gloved hand.

She spoke into the snorkel mouthpiece and delivered one of her favorite Arnold Schwarzenegger lines. "Hasta la vista, kitty!"

Lacey felt relieved as she locked the door and turned to look for Maxwell. Sweaty and wet but feeling accomplished, she was about to remove her foggy mask and step off the front stoop when she heard squealing tires.

EVIL SOLUTIONS

19

EVIL SPIES

Mrs. Wigglesworth thought it was a perfect morning to be riding in her golf cart. Even though she had never golfed a day in her life, she wore a short-sleeved golf shirt with a matching plaid golf skirt. On her head was a plaid driver cap, which she thought looked rather smart. She recalled the words of her late mother, Wahnita Wren Wigglesworth: "Power is perceived. Always look Poweresque."

This was what a well-dressed power cart driver should wear when driving her personalized golf cart around the neighborhood. Mrs. Wigglesworth purchased the cart two years ago when she joined the Society for Women of the Volunteer Neighborhood Watch Committee. She had the cart delivered to Bob's Auto Paint and Repair Shop. Bob did a wonderful job transforming the cart, per her detailed directions.

The reconnaissance golf cart, or ReCon One, was painted army-green camouflage so it would not draw attention in the neighborhood. A bicycle safety flag attached to the roof read "ReCon One". The flag was sewn from camo cloth to blend in and avoid detection. On the back above the license plate,

"Wilma W. Wigglesworth, Volunteering Volunteer" was painted in beautiful gold scroll letters.

It was a sunny day. It was a perfect day for scouting for scoundrels up to no good. Volunteering made Mrs. Wigglesworth swell with pride. The service she was providing for her community was important and powerful. An unsafe neighborhood was the first rung in the ladder leading to chaos and anarchy. Anarchy was not her friend, or for that matter, not even a casual acquaintance.

She turned onto a street with large, older houses and green plush lawns. Wilma had patrolled this street before without incident. She was thinking about what she would have for lunch when she witnessed someone or something exiting a large house on her left.

The small person wore bizarre protective head and face gear with a breathing apparatus and a long trench coat. Trench coat! Breathing apparatus! She slammed on her brakes. Recon One skidded to a stop, positioning her directly across the street from the house and the probable perpetrator.

Through her foggy mask, Lacey saw a camouflage golf cart.
What the—? What the—? A camouflage golf cart? Am I seeing things?

Sweat poured under the bicycle helmet and down both sides of her face.

Mrs. Wigglesworth looked through her binoculars. Her neighborhood watch skills kicked in.

1.Disguise. Young girl wearing a helmet, face mask, and snorkel

2.Dangerous. Beady little eyes shooting daggers directly at her.

3.Criminal clothing. Oversized trench coat.

4. Guilty. Nervous beads of sweat pouring down the girl's face.

5. Tricky. Long, yellow rubber gloves to avoid leaving fingerprints or DNA.

Lacey recognized the woman on the golf cart when she lowered the binoculars from her face.

It's Wigglesworth! What is she doing in a camouflage golf cart and why is she leering at me through binoculars?

Lacey turned her head right to left, trying to locate Maxwell.

Something triggered in Mrs. Wigglesworth's recent memory, a long trench coat, and rubber gloves. She just finished reading an article in *Social Society Magazine* titled "Dangerous Neighborhood Trends." It was about the trend of criminals moving to small towns and setting up their illegal moneymaking in rented houses. Was she witnessing a counterfeit money operation? Was this girl wearing protective gear to work with color dye and print fake money? This was BIG. This was very BIG! She pulled out her cell phone and began taking pictures of the girl to document the evidence.

Lacey's nose was cut off by the swim mask, making it difficult to breathe. She yanked the mask off and saw Mrs. Wigglesworth taking pictures of her with her cell phone camera.

Seriously?

Mrs. Wigglesworth zoomed in and saw the girl's face. "It's Lacey Honeycut!"

Suddenly a male figure appeared next to Lacey. Mrs. Wigglesworth shoved her cellphone in her pocket and floored the gas pedal. Recon One took off. She wasn't about to become the latest person featured on *Unsolvable Mysteries* or appear on an episode of *Coppers*. But maybe Lacey was.

Maxwell said, "There you are! I was getting worried about

you, so I went out back to look in the kitchen window. How did it go? Did my plan work? Did Dr. Evil leave you alone? What's wrong? Cat got your tongue?"

Lacey frowned. "Other than the fact that it's hotter than an Easy-Bake Oven in this getup, it was a complete success!"

"That's great! Then why don't you look happy?"

Lacey pointed in the direction of the escaping camo-cart. "Because SHE'S here again!"

"Mrs. Wigglesworth?"

"Yes, you just missed her reaction to seeing me dressed like this! She was actually staring at me through binoculars and taking pictures of me with her cell phone!"

"What?"

Lacey nodded. "Affirmative, and she was driving some kind of camouflage golf cart!"

Just as Lacey said, "golf cart," a second golf cart zoomed by with two men dressed in golf clothes. One was tall and thin, the other short and plump. They both had bushy mustaches and wore matching shirts and golf visors. Lacey and Maxwell watched them as they passed.

Maxwell said, "More golfers? That's weird. We're not that close to the golf course. I wonder if those two men are following Mrs. Wigglesworth?"

Lacey thought, *or watching us?*

20

CONFUSING CONFESSION

As the cart moved out of sight, both of their walkies sounded with Anna's voice. Anna said, "Walky#1 and #2, come in, this is walky #3. How did the evil kitty caper go? Is anyone injured? Over."

Lacey removed the gloves, hat, and heavy trench coat and handed it all to Maxwell. "I can actually breathe and see again."

She grabbed her walky and pushed the button. "Walky #3. Maxwell's plan worked perfectly! I got the job done. Dr. Evil was too surprised and baffled to bully me! Unfortunately, we had a Wigglesworth sighting. Out."

Anna said, "What? Mrs. Wigglesworth? What does she have to do with Operation Ninja Cat? Out."

Lacey said, "Maxwell and I will catch you up in fifteen minutes. Let's all meet at the Scoop ice cream shop. I need to cool off and I can't think of a better way than ice cream. I have a gift card so it's my treat! Over."

Anna said, "Yummy! I'll see you both there. Over and out."

Mrs. Wigglesworth was spooked. She drove Recon One all the way back home at top speed. It wasn't until she pulled into her own driveway that she felt safe again. Now that she was no longer in harm's way, she was duty-bound to report this immediately. Still seated in her golf cart, she pulled out her cell phone and dialed 911. It was important to remain calm. The emergency operator picked up on the first ring.

Josie Brown had just graduated from 911 emergency call center training. This was her first day to answer the hotline calls on her own. She was prepared for anything. She had a blank legal pad and four No. 2 sharpened pencils sitting on the desk in front of her. Next to the pad was her *Protocol Manual for Intake Calls*, a spiral notebook, and a pre-printed notepad her mother bought her with "My Daughter Rocks" at the top of each page. Josie dreamed of becoming a cop. This job was her first stepping stone to that goal. All she had to do was identify keywords from the caller and follow the flowchart in the 911 Emergency Manual.

Her phone extension rang. Josie answered it on the first ring. "911, this is Josie speaking. Is this an emergency?"

Mrs. Wigglesworth calmly stated, "Yes, this is an emergency."

"Is someone injured or dead?"

"Not yet."

"Are you in imminent danger?"

"Not yet."

"Are you in a safe location?"

Mrs. Wigglesworth looked around her yard. "Yes."

"Please state the nature of your emergency."

"I'm self-reporting illegal money printing."

Josie located the words "self-reporting" on the flowchart. It stated, "CONFESSION, INFORMANT". She followed the suggested course of questioning. "Are you telling me you want to join the law-abiding citizens now?"

"Yes, of course."

Josie thought, this criminal wants to turn herself in. To turn away from her life of crime! I'm fantastic at this job. The flowchart directed her to "gather facts". Josie asked, "Can you provide the location of illegal activity?"

"The address is 6676 Weeping Willow Lane."

Josie thought, Shazam! This counterfeit money bust will get me into the Police Academy. She looked at the flow chart again and read, "reassure the criminal". She said, "Thank you for providing me with the address. You are doing just fine."

"I'm just doing what I must do."

"Exactly. Can you please provide me with your full name and address?"

Mrs. Wigglesworth sighed and thought, this is taking forever. It's never easy doing the right thing. "My name is Wilma Wren Wigglesworth. I live at Turkey Hill Tribute House. It's the stunning Martha Stewart replica home. I'm sure you've seen it in *Luxury Homes Magazine.* It's—"

Josie interrupted. "Mrs. Wigglesworth, may I call you Wilma?" Josie's manual instructed her to "Keep control of the conversation. Ask for names of other criminals and make it personal".

"Yes, of course."

"Thank you. Wilma, is anyone there with you?"

"No, I'm alone."

"Wilma, I know you must feel very alone at this moment."

"I am alone at this moment."

"Yes, I understand. Really, I do. It's never easy to turn in other people."

"We all must take responsibility for our own actions. Especially scoundrels."

Josie searched for the word "responsibility," and saw "obtain a confession,". "Wilma, are you confessing to me that you were at the fake money house today?"

"Yes, I told you I was there." Wilma thought, this 911 operator isn't the sharpest crayon in the box.

"Wilma, would you like to give me the names of the others in your group?"

"She's not in my group, but Lacey Honeycut was there and I was there with Recon1."

Josie heard Recon One and followed the flow chart to "gang names". Was Josie uncovering gang activity right here in the small town of Meriwether Pines? Was this Lacey Honeycut the gang leader? Was Recon One a code name? Josie's heart started pounding like crazy. She did not feel qualified to deal with this.

The flowchart stated, "Gang activity. Disconnect and contact the supervisor. Before disconnecting, praise the caller for taking the first step, emphasizing police protection. Report the criminal to your supervisor."

In a squeaky, nervous voice, Josie said, "Mrs. Wigglesworth, I would like to praise you for taking the initiative today to—as you called it, self-report. I know it can be uncomfortable, but it's vital to report these things before someone gets hurt or worse."

"Yes, this is my thought as well."

"I want to assure you that you will be eligible for police protection and possibly witness relocation."

"Well, I have no plans on moving away from my Turkey Hill Tribute House, but I certainly hope the police will protect this neighborhood."

"Definitely, Wilma, this is beyond the scope of my job

description. Someone who is in a better position to assist you will be contacting you soon. Does that make sense?"

"Yes, that makes sense."

"Wilma, thank you for doing the right thing and have a safe day."

"Thank you."

Mrs. Wigglesworth disconnected the call and thought, that went quite well. I reported that Lacey Honeycut criminal to 911. Maybe I'll receive a good citizen accommodation.

Josie disconnected the call and thought, that went quite well.

I'll report this Wigglesworth criminal to my supervisor. Maybe I'll receive a 911 accommodation.

Mrs. Wigglesworth headed inside.

The two men in the golf cart watched her entering her home through their long-range observation binoculars. The shorter man sent a text to his Washington office. "We've got surveillance on the woman who filed the Hazardous Air Report."

The response came back. "Is she connected to the illegal money scheme?"

21

MARSHMALLOW WINNER

As Mrs. Wigglesworth walked into the living room, her cell phone started to play *We Are the Champions* by Queen. This song alerted her to eBay auctions. The song that was all about winning and power was letting her know that an eBay auction was ending. She sat in her rocker and opened the eBay app. "Ending soon, Item 2348t6 Authentic Michelle Obama Etched Giant Marshmallow."

Mrs. Wigglesworth was an avid eBay auction winner. She proudly displayed artifacts and tributes to sophisticated and important women of power in an illuminated glass case in her living room. This would make a perfect addition to her memorabilia. A giant marshmallow with the face of Michelle Obama seared on it. She admired the former First Lady of the United States. She had to own it at any cost! The app was counting down. With only seconds left, she entered a preposterously high dollar bid and held her breath.

"Auction Ended. You won!"

The words flashed on her phone. It was hers! She was now the proud owner of a genuine marshmallow tribute to Michelle

Obama, unlike any other. Fantastic! What a morning this had been. First, she quashed Lacey Honeycut's life of crime and now this lucky acquisition. It was time to celebrate with a cup of Martha Stewart ginseng-and-honey tea.

Still sitting in their golf cart, Special FBI Agents Smith and Smith received another text from the Washington office with a report attached "Guess who just placed a 911 call and wants to confess to being part of a money counterfeiting ring?"

Agent Smith texted back. "Mrs. Wigglesworth?"

TING.

The reply came back. "Affirmative. Review the report and proceed to arrest."

Agent Smith said, "Fantastic! What a morning this had been. First, we locate a person possibly filing false air pollution reports and now that same person confesses to a crime."

Agent Smith said, "This is a lucky assignment."

*We Are the Champi*ons started playing again on Mrs. Wigglesworth's phone. Another eBay auction that she didn't want to miss. Margaret Thatcher's toothbrush was being auctioned. Margaret Thatcher, the FIRST female Prime Minister of the United Kingdom, the Iron Lady; now that was a woman of POWER! The Iron Lady used this toothbrush! It contains her DNA. Money was no object. Mrs. Wigglesworth was bidding to win.

Ding dong

Mrs. Wigglesworth thought I wonder who that could be? She opened her door. Two men wearing matching golf clothes stood in front of her.

"Yes, can I help you?"

The tall man with a bushy mustache said, "We're here regarding your 911 call."

Mrs. Wigglesworth was impressed. "I only placed that call minutes ago. I need to make a larger contribution next year to the Meriwether Pines Police Charity. You guys are fast."

The short, stout man said, "We're not police officers."

Mrs. Wigglesworth's eyes narrowed to a small line. "Then who are you?"

Short mustache man said, "We're FBI agents."

Wilma let out a chortle. "Dressed as golfers? I need to see some identification."

Tall and thin said, "Show her your ID. I left mine at the hotel."

Short and stout pulled out a small thin leather wallet, flipped it open and held it up for Mrs. Wigglesworth to see.

She read the ID card, "Meriwether Pines Miniature Golf Membership Card?"

Shorty's face turned tomato red. He plucked the golf card out, revealing his FBI badge behind it. "Sorry, my wife says I'm unorganized. As you can see, I'm Agent Smith and this is my partner, Agent Smith. We need to come in and speak with you about your confession."

Mrs. Wigglesworth's hands flew to her mouth. "Confession? I made no confession."

Agent Smith said, "Please step aside and allow us to conduct our investigation."

Mrs. Wigglesworth let them in and walked them into her kitchen.

Agent Smith said, "Please sit down. We have some questions for you about counterfeiting."

Agent Smith said, "We also want to talk with you about Lacey Honeycut, the other criminal in your Recon One gang."

Mrs. Wigglesworth sank into her kitchen chair and thought, I'm in big trouble.

22

SCOOBY MYSTERY

Anna was already waiting at the Scoop when they arrived and waved them over to sit at the outside table. It was the lime sherbet table. Each table at The Scoop was named after an ice cream flavor. An umbrella covered with lime green emoji faces shaded their large slice of lime table. Lacey and Maxwell plopped onto ice-cream cone chairs.

Lacey said, "Important stuff first, Anna, what do you want?"

"My usual, vanilla double scoop cone with chocolate sprinkles."

Maxwell said, "I'll take the Anna-banana split, ha-ha, with extra chocolate sauce and walnuts."

Lacey placed their orders and gave the girl her gift card. "I'll have an Oreo cookie milkshake."

Anna helped Lacey carry the containers of frozen happiness to their table.

Lacey raised her milkshake cup to her friends and said, "Here's to Maxwell and his Dr. Evil protective gear!"

Anna said, "Here's to eating ice-cream before lunch!"

In between scarfing down mouthfuls of his banana split,

Maxwell caught Anna up on the visit with Dr. Evil and Shadow. Lacey interjected along the way with colorful descriptions of her own. Everyone was concerned about Mrs. Wigglesworth's spying behavior and the strange men on the golf cart.

Lacey said, "Ever since she saw Mickey and fell into the pool—"

"That was heee-larious." Said, Anna.

"I agree." Said Lacey. "But it feels like she's going out of her way to cause trouble for me."

Anna said, "She's stalking you. Aren't there laws against that? Should we call the police?"

Lacey and Maxwell both barked, "No!"

Anna wiped some sprinkles from her mouth. The ice cream was melting faster than frosty the snowman. "Okay, okay, no police."

Lacey said, "I think too many wonky Wigglesworth scuff-ups are making me wacky. Maybe the strange men are her friends."

Maxwell said, "Friends who follow her around on golf carts?"

"This is better than a Scooby-Doo mystery." Said Anna.

Lacey said, "I love Scooby but I don't want to be in a mystery."

Anna said, "I agree. By the way, my mom and I picked the place for my birthday party. We checked out Wild Kangaroo Land trampoline park. The complex is massive! They took us on a tour. We saw indoor villages, go-carts, zip lines, and climbing walls. Everything was lit with black lights so the neon colors glow in the dark." She opened up her beach bag and pulled out two neon-yellow envelopes. "For your delight, here's the invites. There'll be cake, games, and fun. You can shoot me with a laser gun."

Maxwell looked at his invitation. "I'm psyched! That place is new. It just opened up last month. My friend Mike had his birthday there but I couldn't go—science convention. He said it's *reeedunkulous*."

Lacey said, "Anna, I can't wait! It will be a blast!"

Anna sighed. "By the way, I had to invite Jimmy."

Lacey rolled her eyes. "Ugh, why does he have to come? He's a year younger than us."

"True, but because he skipped a grade, he's in our class. Then there's the small fact that he's my cousin."

Maxwell said, "That skinny kid who always cries about everything? He's a total pain in the pancreas!"

Anna sympathized. "I know guys. He's a major twerp, but

he's my cousin. My mom is making me invite him. We'll just have to deal."

Maxwell wiped his mouth and said, "I'd better get going. I need to return the baby trailer to my neighbor. I've got a NASA Geeks Skype meeting at noon. The subject is 'How to get recommendations from teachers for the Space Camp scholarship.'"

Anna said, "Fill us in on that. You know it's all three of us or no deal! I've got to skedaddle too. My mom is trimming my hair today at her shop. My bangs are so long I can barely see. Walky-talky up and stay connected."

Back at Wilma Wigglesworth's house, the interrogation was just beginning.

23

ARRESTING DEVELOPMENTS

Agent Smith said, "We are here to discover what you may or may not know about a counterfeit money organization."

Confused, Wilma said, "I only know what I saw."

Agent Smith said, "For purposes of multiple penal codes and several federal regulations, I cannot disperse any new information to you."

Wilma asked, "Then, why are you here?"

Agent Smith said, "We are here to arrest you and round up the other members of your Recon One gang."

"Arrest me? What gang? That's the name of my golf cart."

Agent Smith said, "Per code 543a subsection C, WE ask the questions here."

GULP.

Wigglesworth closed her mouth and swallowed an invisible frog.

Silence.

Agent Smith pulled out his cell phone and swiped the screen. The other Agent Smith pulled out a small laser pointer pen. Tall Smith showed a picture on the cell phone to Wilma as

Short Smith pointed the laser beam at the photo. (A high-tech FBI multi-media production.)

"Do you know this girl?"

In a shaky voice, the interviewee replied, "That's Lacey Honeycut."

Short Smith moved the laser pointer around the photos like some kind of low budget laser light show.

"Is she a member of your criminal gang?

"She probably is in a gang, but not mine."

"So, you admit that you're in a gang?"

Mrs. Wigglesworth sat up tall and lifted her strong chin. "Now you listen to me. I am not in a gang. I am one of the most respected citizens of Meriwether Pines. I was reporting a crime!" She scowled at the golfing agents and thought, I've had just about enough of Tweedle short and Tweedle Tall.

Wilma Wigglesworth stood up and said, "I've had just about enough of you two. I'm calling my lawyer."

The Agents looked at each other with an if-she-calls-her-lawyer-the-boys-in-the-Washington-office-will-have-our-heads, look.

Agent Smith said, "Please have a seat. I'm sure we can get to the bottom of this."

"I will not sit down. It's time for you both to leave."

Ting.

Agent Smith read his text out loud. "They have cleared Lacey Honeycut. She's simply an eleven-year-old girl who was dealing with a bad kitty. She's running her friend's pet sitting business and had permission to be at that home."

"Cleared?!! Honeycut?!!!" Mrs. Wigglesworth looked like her head was going to rotate full circle, explode into flames and blast off through the roof of her beloved Martha Stewart home.

"That's it!" She thrust her arm out and pointed to her front door. "Get out of here!"

Agent Smith looked at Agent Smith with a, we-should-go-now look on his face.

Agent Smith said, "We'll follow up with you—."

"—I said GET OUT!"

The two golfers moved quickly, narrowly escaping the slamming door.

Mrs. Wigglesworth stood fuming at her window, watching them leave. She thought, if they will not arrest Lacey Honeycut, then I must take this into my own hands.

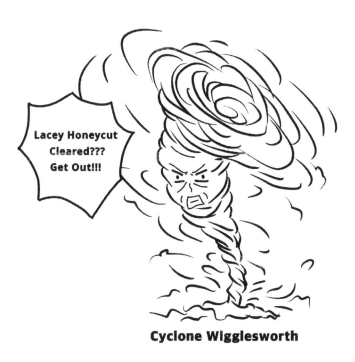

Cyclone Wigglesworth

24

NAKED BOOGER

The following morning, Lacey stood in front of a two-story house. After all the drama with Dr. Evil, Lacey hoped this critter client would be easy-peasy. She pulled Charlotte's file book out. On the form, the box marked "DOG" was checked with a number three written next to it. Other boxes checked were "WALK", "WATER", and "TREATS."

I'm walking three dogs!

Next to dogs' names, it said, "Stella, Brutus, and Booger."

Booger! That's hilarious. I wonder what a dog named Booger looks like?

Her eyes scanned the form for the file note at the bottom of the form. Charlotte had squiggled,

_ohair____screen poor _feet.

Lacey looked up to the sky and shouted out loud, "Why? Charlotte? Why can't you write a file note that makes any sense?" Somehow shouting at no one made her feel better. She put on her Crittercam cap, unlocked the large front door, and stepped into the huge foyer.

A large staircase with high vaulted ceilings divided the

entryway. Everything was white. White carpet, white couches with white throw pillows, white glossy picture frames, and white flower vases sat on matching white side tables.

Someone likes white.

High above the staircase was a giant portrait of a blonde woman with her hair in a bun on top of her head. She was wearing a red business suit and sitting on a large brown wingback chair. Three furless dogs sat with the woman.

Jinkies! THREE Chinese Crested hairless dogs!

The one in the center looked more like a small rat than a dog.

I've read about Chinese Crested hairless dogs but I've never seen one in person. This will be awesome!

To her right was a white box with assorted dog clothes including t-shirts, raincoats, and sweaters. There were also several bottles of spray mist sunblock and mosquito repellant. She located three sets of harnesses with leashes hanging on the wall.

Lacey heard dogs barking upstairs. "Who Let the Dogs Out?"

Lacey giggled. "I love that song!"

She took the harnesses and leashes with her up the large staircase singing "woof, woof, woof". Lacey turned to her left at the top of the stairs and followed the sound of yapping dogs.

She opened the bedroom door and couldn't believe her eyes. In front of her were the wackiest, ugliest, cutest dogs she had ever seen. Two of the Chinese Crested dogs surrounded her, jumping and yapping—yapping and jumping. They weren't entirely furless. Each one had a wild shock of hair on top of their heads and little tufts on their feet and tails. Their skin was covered with freckles and they wore t-shirts.

Lacey guessed the largest dog was Stella because she had on a pink t-shirt that read "Princess Pups Rule". Stella danced around Lacey on her two back feet like a wild child.

Boing, boing

She bounced up and down like a pogo stick with tufts of white-blonde hair flapping in front of her brown eyes.

Rooby Roo! These dogs are Rilarious!

Next to Stella another mostly bald pup showed his enthusiasm by bouncing; Pick me! Pick me! He wore a black t-shirt with the words "Snarky & Barky".

"You must be Brutus. You just don't look like a Booger."

Lacey sat down cross-legged on the floor to greet them at

their own level. She learned this from watching five million episodes of *The Dog Whisperer*. Both happy pooches immediately tried to jump on her lap at the same time. She pet one with each hand.

"Hi, Stella and Brutus. I'm Lacey. You are both insanely adorable! Who needs fur when you're this cute!" Brutus leaped up and licked Lacey's face. Lacey laughed and wiped the slobber off her cheek with her sleeve.

"Thank you for the kisses!" She flipped him on his back and settled him on her lap to tickle his belly. This technique allowed her to wrangle Brutus and Stella into their harnesses.

Now, where is Booger?

25

BOOGER PROBLEMS

Lacey looked around the room for dog number three. She spotted him sheltering next to the bed. He was one of the most pitiful creatures Lacey had ever laid eyes on. Booger was much tinier than the other dogs. He looked like a cross between an alien and a wrinkled old man. His frail little legs bowed inward and shook with fear. His head was proportionally too tiny for his body. Two shy brown eyes peered out between thin pieces of hair. Lacey's heart broke. She loved him instantly.

She slowly scooched over to him and held her hand out so he could smell it. When he seemed satisfied with the greeting, she smoothed his hair out of his eyes. In a soft voice, she cooed, "Hi little Booger. I'm Lacey Honeycut, your summer dog walker. You're okay buddy." Booger stopped shaking and took a tentative step closer to her.

She scooped him up into her arms. He was wearing a cute little navy and red t-shirt that said "Personal Trainer". Lacey laughed and hugged him. "Okay, Booger, let's get this party started. I'll put your harness on and we'll all go for a walk."

Lacey carried Booger down with Brutus and Stella following

her. At the door, she realized the sunscreen was for the dogs. She knew from reading about this breed they get sunburns easy because they don't have fur. She sprayed all three dogs with sunscreen around their t-shirts.

As soon as they got out in the front yard, Lacey realized *this is going to be a challenge.* Not only was she trying to control three different leashes at once, but Booger refused to walk. Stella and Brutus were ready to go. They were pulling at the end of their leashes and bucking like wild horses, Yee-haw let's go!

They're so excited and happy to be outside. Actually, they were just as excited and happy when they were inside—just two naked dogs, happy wherever they went.

Meanwhile, on the other side of the world, poor little Booger had planted himself firmly by the front door with an I'm-not-going-anywhere look on his tiny face. His skinny front legs pointing inward had started trembling again. When Lacey tried to walk back toward Booger to comfort him, Stella and Brutus decided it was a good time to turn and run a circle around her legs.

I'm lassoed.

As she attempted to free herself from the leashes of death, she looked at Booger. What a sad sight he was! Lacey's heart just broke for him. She called out "Booger, it's okay. I'm trying to reach you. I'll be right there." Lacey untangled herself and picked up Booger. Nestling him in the nook of her left elbow, she said, "Okay, little buddy, I think you're going to have to ride the Lacey taxi."

While holding the other two leashes with her right hand, she could walk Stella and Brutus down the street. When she got to the halfway point to turn around, she placed Booger on the grass. "Okay, Mr. Booger, this is your time to shine."

Booger did his duty. Stella and Brutus were already pulling in the other direction to head back home. Lacey carried Booger all the way back. By the time they got back, her left arm was numb from holding him and the other dogs were doing impressions of a twisted pretzel.

This is impossible! There has to be a better way to do this!

Lacey took their leashes off, gave them treats and refilled their water bowls.

"I'll see you pups in a few days." Lacey locked the huge front door.

I need advice from Team Critter on this three-dog-dilemma. We need a solution for walking two marathon runners and one slow sloth at the same time. While I'm getting their help on Operation Booger, I will suggest Operation Wigglesworth.

26

EXPLODING ARREST

The morning sun lit up Wilma Wigglesworth's living room as she paced and mumbled, mumbled and paced. "Honeycut cleared, humph! I know she's up to something."

She paused in front of the large chalkboard on the wall that had kept her up the night before. It was now filled with her plans to get Lacey Honeycut and shut down her friend's pet sitting business. "I'm taking Recon One out and I will patrol the neighborhood until I find her!"

She carried her bag with surveillance equipment out to Recon One. Dressed for battle, her camouflage pants and shirt matched the camouflage paint on the cart. She took off on the cart at full speed. "Failure is not an option."

Another golf cart was also camouflaged, but with real bushes, branches, and leaves.

Agent Smith said, "She's on the move. Clear away the golf cart's disguise and let's go."

Agent Smith tugged at a large branch. "I can't get it all off."

"Forget it. We can't lose her."

A bush sped off chasing Recon One.

Mrs. Wigglesworth had no idea she was being followed. As the afternoon turned to dusk, she drove up and down one street after another looking for hooligans. A Lacey hooligan. The streets grew dark. She switched on her headlights and specially designed searchlight.

A red porch light caught her eye, and she slowed down in front of the house, whispering to herself. "The article I read said that criminals sometimes identify their houses to other criminals by using colored lightbulbs."

She stopped her cart and saw a figure exiting the garage door. The person wore long rubber gloves.

Just as the FBI's traveling bush-cart arrived, Mrs. Wigglesworth launched herself from Recon One, running and screaming like a wild woman. "Lacey Honeycut! I know it's you!"

The figure froze in the driveway.

Agent Smith said, "What is she doing?"

Wigglesworth grabbed the person's hand. "Lacey, I caught you red-handed."

A young man's face looked at her. He yanked his hand away, leaving Wilma clutching an empty rubber glove. The one-gloved man sprinted back into the house through the garage.

Wigglesworth was too shocked to move.

Smith and Smith jumped out of their bush and ran towards the house.

Agent Smith said, "You take Wilma. I'll look for the other person."

Agent Smith looked at her camouflage outfit and shook his head. "Wilma Wigglesworth, place your hands behind your head and walk in front of me to my golf cart."

Wilma put her hands behind her head and then looked around for his cart. Confused, she looked at him.

Agent Smith pointed. "The cart that looks like a bush."

The other Agent Smith came running out of the garage, pulling the young man behind him. "Everybody run! The house is rigged with explosives and it's going to blow!"

Two Smiths, one Wigglesworth, and an unnamed counterfeiter ducked down behind a cart-bush.

Boom! Boom!

Two loud explosions ignited the house on fire.

Agent Smith dialed 911. "This is FBI Agent Smith, badge number 444, calling in a house fire." He gave the location and basics to the 911 operator while still holding onto the suspect's arm. "Let's take these two to the police station."

Shorty Smith pulled more branches off the back seat of the cart and moved his golf bag to the back rack. He directed the unhappy guy. "Sit down." He whispered to Tall Smith, "Ever since we left the police force and became FBI agents, we hardly ever make any arrests."

Tall Smith whispered, "That was kind of fun." He helped Mrs. Wigglesworth into the back seat next to the man.

"What are we going to use to tie their hands?"

"Where are your favorite handcuffs, Shock and Awe?"

"I didn't think I'd need them on a golf cart. I didn't even bring my gun."

"Dig around in the golf bag and see if you can find anything."

Agent Smith rifled through the golf bag and pulled out two sweat headbands. "Will this work?"

"Tie their hands together. That should hold them till we get to the police station."

Mrs. Wigglesworth protested. "Why are you tying me to a criminal and what are you arresting ME for?"

"We are arresting you for interfering with Federal Officers. Do you have anything else that you want to confess to?

27

HORSING AROUND

After the Booger rodeo, Lacey went to Huntclub. After her chores, she said, "It's Sir Lancelot time!"

Sir Lancelot was a famous knight who was very brave and handsome. Lacey thought Lancelot was brave when he took her over high jumps. He was a handsome chestnut-colored horse with white points and a perfect white elongated star on his forehead. She patted his head and gave him a carrot. "Sir Lancelot, are you ready to ride?"

Lacey bridled him up and led him out to the field. She saw the twins Vanessa and Valencia riding their horses in the field next to the stalls. They were riding in the flat grassy meadow, having fun playing with their horses outside of the training rings. The twins urged their horses on to a fast gallop, then slowed them down to trot.

She didn't know the girls well because they were older than her and attended a private school. They were entering seventh grade next year. Valencia and Vanessa were identical twins. They had wide-set green eyes framed by light brown, naturally curly long hair. Lacey and Maxwell came up with the nickname

"V-squared" for them.

The twins attended Sacred Holy Innocence Catholic School and lived in a huge mansion near the golf course. They didn't have to rent their horses like Lacey did. They had a pair of pure white Thoroughbred Shagya Arabians. This breed of horse is considered to be excellent at competing in dressage. The girls named them Isadora and Isabella. Lacey thought the horses were stunning. She walked Lancelot out to the gate and asked if she could join in.

Vanessa said, "Sure, come on in. Let's see how responsive he is to your commands." Lacey spent the next hour with the twins. They took turns giving her tips and helping her with Lancelot.

Valencia said, "Sometimes rental horses can be more stubborn to control. The problem is they have so many riders at different levels of capability. So sometimes they take advantage of the situation."

Lacey was standing next to Lancelot while he cooled down after the workout. "I've heard that before. Mrs. Goodall is thinking about selling Lancelot. I'm hoping to buy him. I've been saving my money."

They started walking their horses back up to the stalls when Vanessa said, "It is nice to have your own horse. I'll keep my fingers crossed for you and for Lancelot. It's obvious he is very bonded to you."

Lacey said, "Thanks for all your help today. He's already listening better."

That evening, Lacey sat in her bedroom, scrutinizing Charlotte's latest postcard. The front showed the London Eye, "Europe's Tallest Ferris Wheel". She flipped the postcard over. In very neat block letters, Charlotte wrote, "I finally made it to London with Uncle Conway. We rode the London Eye! Isn't my handwriting better? By the way, Booger can't walk very well. Miss you all!"

Lacey laughed. *Seriously Charlotte?*

She picked up her walky.

I hope they'll go along with my Wigglesworth plan.

28

BOOGER SOLUTIONS

Lacey recounted her Booger story and told them about Charlotte's postcard.

Anna giggled. "Charlotte, the great, it seems her fate is to always be late. How will we ever compensate? Out."

Maxwell commented, "Walky #3, nice one Banana. Out."

Lacey said, "Walky #3, Anna put that clever rhyming brain of yours to use. Any Booger ideas, people? Out."

Anna said, "Hey, I've got a perfect solution for Booger!" Before she could finish, Maxwell cut her off.

"Walky #3, please remember your protocol. Out."

"Oh brother, walkies #1 and #2, Are you happy now Maxwell? Listen up Critter Team! This is my solution! Booger skates! We'll make tiny roller skates for him so he can keep up with Stella and Brutus. What ya' think? Over."

Lacey queried back, "Walky #3, what if he crashes? Over."

Forgetting the protocol, Anna piped back. "We'll sew mini shin-guards and wrist-guards for him and make a tiny crash helmet. And on his shirt, we can write 'Make way for Booger'. Over."

Maxwell had to say something. He thought Anna's idea was preposterous, and she was going full steam ahead with it. He had to put the brakes on before she took it any further and signed Booger up for a roller hockey league. "Walkies #2 and #3, let's come back to the planet Earth. We need to come up with an idea that is viable. We need to approach this like a science problem."

"Fact 1, we have a Booger."

"Fact 2, we have a Booger who is not fully mobile."

"Fact 3, we need to help the Booger get mobile without injuring him in the process."

"A few minutes of radio silence please, while I think! Over."

Anna decided not to get her feelings hurt after Maxwell shot her idea down in flames.

Anna and Lacey commenced radio silence. They had known Maxwell long enough to understand his process for problem-solving. It wasn't the friendliest or the politest. His thinking was methodical and scientific. HE was methodical and scientific.

That being said, he delivered results—which is why Maxwell was named "Galaxy Explorer of the Year" by the Academy of Future Astronauts of America, three years in a row. Wernher is the reason Maxwell was not the winner four years in a row. That's why he kept an X'd-out picture of Einstein Albert Wernher's trophy in the Trias-Lab.

During the five-minute radio silence, which seemed like five years, Lacey sat on her bed petting Drowsy and looking at the London Eye postcard. She'd love to ride it someday and see London.

Anna was pacing back and forth in her bedroom, trying to recover from the rejection of her innovative Booger roller derby proposal. Anna considered herself an arteest. She was highly creative and artistically gifted. She stood in front of her full-length mirror and put her hands on her hips.

"Anna, your idea was ingenious, even if nobody else realizes it."

Her reflection stared back at her, nodding her head and looking extremely cute. She spoke again to the cute girl in the mirror. "I'll just write it down in my 'Book of Ideas' journal along with all my other brilliant schemes."

Maxwell broke the silence. "Walkies #1 and #3, I've got it. Anna, your idea wasn't completely out of the solar system."

Anna made a face in the mirror and whispered, "No, Dah!"

Maxwell continued. "I was able to derive a basic premise from it and incorporate a more viable solution. I've run the stats through my brainpan and we're good to go. I'll get working on the design right away. The prototype will be ready for testing at Lacey's next appointment. Booger will go from drool to cool. Over"

"Perfect.", said Lacey. "Now I need to talk to you both about Wigglesworth. I suggest we use Mickey, wearing his remote-controlled harness to execute Liberandum-Surveillance at Wigglesworth's house. We need to get in there and see what's going on. Over."

Anna said, "You're going to use the secret rescue mouse training word?"

"That's right. Liberandum, the Latin word for rescue. All of Mickey's Trias lab training will finally get tested in the real world. Over."

Maxwell said, "Are you sure you really want to send him into her house?"

Lacey said, "It's risky, but yes."

Anna said, "Count me in. Over."

Maxwell said, "Walkies #2 and #3, Lacey can put the plan together and email it to us. I'm in too! Gotta go. Over and Out"

Anna's voice came back on. "Not over and out yet. News flash! Here's an important reminder. TOMORROW is my Jumping Wild Kangaroo birthday party extravaganza. Be there or be square. Now it's over and out."

Lacey put her walky back on the charger.

I've been so busy, I forgot to buy Anna's birthday present!

29

TUFF LOVE

Lacey grabbed her wallet and Charlotte's backpack and passed Mom in the kitchen. "Be back in a few."

"Okay, we're having dinner in an hour. Don't be late."

Lacey jumped on her bike and pedaled toward the bookstore.

They have really zany-kooky cards there and maybe I'll get her a photography book.

Six blocks from her house, she saw an old lady walking a Jack Russell terrier mix. The cute, scruffy dog was yipping and pulling on his leash like a beagle ready for a foxhunt.

BEEEEEEP! BEEEEEEP!

A black motorcycle flashed on Lacey's left and plowed right through the stop sign without stopping. The lady walking the dog startled as her dog went ballistic trying to attack the escaping daredevil. She lost her grip on the leash and the irate rascal ran into the middle of the intersection, barking like a madman; I dare you to take me on!

A second thunderous motorcycle chasing at a higher rate of speed appeared and barreled directly at the wound-up pup.

Everything seemed to move in slow motion. Lacey heard the lady screaming.

"TUFFY! TUFFY!"

In an attempt to stop and rescue the dog, Lacey slammed on her brakes. Her bike came to an abrupt stop, but she kept going, launching over the handlebars like a rocket.

THWOMP

Her bare knees hit the pavement and she could feel skin ripping away as she careened into the intersection directly in the path of the speeding chopper.

THUD

The high-pitched barking ended with one painful screeching whine and a whimper that Lacey would never forget. The roaring engine never even slowed. As the bundle of fur and bones tumbled directly in front of Lacey, the deadly driver disappeared down the road.

Lacey heard a muffled yelp and turned her attention back to the crumpled creature. One terrified brown eye gazed at Lacey in shock as small drops of blood fell from its nose and dribbled from the side of a wide-open mouth and lolling tongue.

TUFFY!

The owner yelled his name then stood frozen in shock by the stop sign. Lacey leaned in close to the dog's head and whispered, "Tuffy, you're okay buddy."

She placed her hand gingerly on the now trembling little head.

"Everything will be okay."

Lacey had to act quickly. She looked in all directions of the intersection, but there wasn't another person or car in sight. The old lady managed to shuffle over to them. She clutched her hands over her mouth and began to cry hysterically.

I've got to get Tuffy to the Merri Vet.

The Merri Vet clinic was only four blocks away. It was a place Lacey knew well because she used to volunteer there. Lacey stood up and placed her now shaking hands on the woman's arms.

"I'm taking Tuffy to the Merri Vet. Everything will be okay."

The woman just stared at her through tear-filled eyes. Lacey didn't know if she was listening, but getting the dog help was her number one priority.

"Meet me there."

Lacey removed her backpack and unzipped it. She opened it wide next to the injured dog. He was still breathing, but he looked really terrible. He let out a sharp cry of pain as Lacey gingerly moved him into the backpack. She left the top partially open and strapped it to the front of her chest.

Thank God my bike is still working.

With tears streaming down her face, her bleeding legs pushed as fast as they could.

The Merri Vet had one car parked out front but the door was locked. Lacey looked at Tuffy. His entire body was trembling.

He's going into shock.

His eyes were closed but somehow, he was still breathing.

BANG! BANG! BANG! BANG!

Lacey pounded on the door and screamed at the top of her lungs. "This is an EMERGENCY! Please let us in! Hello! Can anyone hear me?"

BANG! BANG! BANG! BANG!

She saw a bell and pushed it repeatedly until a face appeared in the window. It was Dr. Debby.

She's still here!

The door swung open and Lacey opened the backpack wide.

"I think he might die! A motorcycle hit him."

At the sight of Dr. Debby, Lacey cried even harder, which made it impossible to explain any further. Dr. Debby carefully lifted the unconscious pup from the bag and put her ear to his chest. "He's still alive. Sit in the waiting room and I'll do what I can."

"Please don't let him die."

"I'll do my best Lacey. What's his name?"

Through sobs, she said, "Tuffy. Little Tuffy."

Lacey sat down in the waiting room. Both of her knees were scraped raw with bits of dirt and pavement sticking to the drying blood. Her heart was pounding wildly.

Please God, let him be okay.

The door opened again and Dr. Debby stood there in her scrubs.

"Lacey, both of my assistants are not answering their phones. Tuffy needs help now. Can you pull yourself together and assist me in surgery?"

Lacey wiped away the tears from her cheeks and stood up.

30

LACEY'S MISSING

Lacey was hardly ever late for dinner, but sometimes she lost track of time. She was the kind of kid that Sara never had to worry about. That's why it took so long for the alarm bells to ring in her head when Lacey failed to show up for dinner. After bathing Petey and reading him a story, she went downstairs to make sure Lacey was eating the dinner she left for her. No Lacey. Her bike wasn't in the garage and she wasn't anywhere in the house. Sara ran into Steve's office.

"Lacey never came home."

Steve was working on his computer. "I'm sure she'll be back soon, it's only—"

"—It's ten-thirty!"

Steve looked at Sara and his face turned white. "You get Petey and I'll get the car started."

Now it was close to midnight and Lacey's mom was trying her best not to panic as she drove up and down the neighborhood roads looking for her daughter's bicycle or any signs of Lacey. Steve sat next to her as Petey slept in his car seat.

"Sara, I think we're going to have to consider calling some

of her friends to see if she is with them."

"It's midnight."

"I know and I'm not trying to alarm you even more, but this is getting serious. We might even want to consider calling the police."

Sara held her hand to her mouth, trying her best not to cry. "Where is she!"

Steve picked up his cell phone. "Should I try Anna's house first?"

Sara slowed down and took inventory of where she was. They were almost back at the house now. She had an idea. "Let me try one more place. Lacey used to volunteer at a vet clinic and she always spent tons of time there."

She made a U-turn and sped in the direction of the Merri Vet Clinic. The lights were on in the clinic and two cars were parked out front. Lacey's bicycle was lying in the parking lot on its side.

"She's here! Steve, maybe she's hurt!"

Sara ran into the clinic. An old lady and a younger man sat in the waiting room.

"Have you seen the girl who was riding that bicycle outside?"

The man stood up and said, "Yes, she's in there."

Steve followed in holding Petey who was still sleeping. "Is she here?"

The old lady said, "Your daughter is with Tuffy."

Sara was confused and exhausted. "Tuffy?"

The man explained. "My mom's dog got hit and your daughter brought him here for emergency care."

The double doors suddenly swung open with a creaking sound. Everyone turned to see Dr. Debby and Lacey wearing scrubs.

In a shaky voice, the lady said, "Tuffy?"

Dr. Debby said, "It was touch and go, but you gave him the right name. He's strong, and he will make it."

The woman started sobbing. Her son comforted her.

Dr. Debby turned to Sara and Steve. "You've got a very special eleven-year-old daughter."

They headed for the door with their arms around her and both said, "We know."

As they exited the vet clinic, a highly agitated Wilma Wigglesworth exited jail.

31

BIRTHDAY SPIES

The next afternoon, Wild Kangaroo Land trampoline park was packed with partygoers and their parents dropping them off. They gathered in the front entrance where a scrolling LED sign read "Anna's Birthday Party, Jump Till You Drop!"

Two Wild Roo staff members addressed the group. They spoke with fake Australian accents (for an authentic Australian experience). The boy and girl were high school age. They wore matching neon-blue collared golf-style shirts with khaki pants. Their shirts read, "Let's get wild!" with a cartoon drawing of a smiling kangaroo jumping on a trampoline. They motioned for the group to follow them down the hall. They all filed into the Jumping Jukebox Café.

The girl spoke first. "G'day mates." "I've traveled from the Land of Down Under for this special occasion. Welcome to Anna's birthday bash. I'm really stoked to get this going. Let's bring the birthday girl up to the front of the room. Where are you, Anna?"

Anna, who was never shy but was short enough to get lost in the crowd, started jumping up and down, waving her arms.

The girl Wild Roo said, "There you are. Come on up."

Anna ran up to stand in between the Wild Roos. Girl Roo placed a sparkling neon "Birthday Queen" tiara on Anna's head. Anna's face lit up with a huge grin from ear to ear.

The boy handed Anna two large neon, yellow paper bags with handles. Absolutely everything was neon at The Wild Kangaroo. He said, "Anna, this is your birthday party so you get to pick the teams. We have twenty kids so pick ten for each team including you. Have a go at it but make sure to include Blokes and Sheilas on both teams."

Anna, who was not versed in Australian lingo, looked confused. "Blokes and Sheilas?"

Girl Wild Roo exclaimed, "Crikey, so sorry, that's what we call boys and girls down under in Australia."

Lacey thought, *they really take this Australian experience thing seriously at Wild Kangaroo Land.*

Anna gave two thumbs up. "Got it!".

Girl Roo continued, "While we explain the rules, Anna will hand out these neon shirts. If Anna hands you a neon, green shirt, you're on the Leaping Lizards team. Those who get the neon, orange shirt, are Flying Squirrels. Put the shirts on over your clothes and you'll glow like everything else in the main stage." Anna handed out the shirts to pick teams.

Boy Roo raised his voice so everyone could hear. "The birthday tournament has three competitions. At the end of the contests, the team with the most points will win. The first event is the Zippyroo. You will be zip-lining over glow-in-the-dark trampoline targets. You decide when to let go and aim for a target. You must land inside of the target on the trampoline trail in order to score a point for your team."

One kid yelled, "What if I miss the target?"

Boy Roo said, "If you land outside the target, you'll still bounce, but no score."

A girl in the back shouted, "What if I don't jump?"

Miss. Roo said, "If you don't jump along the way, you will land in a bouncy pool full of balls and get zero points for your team. Everyone will wear a safety helmet, so no worries mates, you'll just boing, boing like a kangaroo. Have fun and remember all of Wild Kangaroo Land is covered by cameras so we can monitor team scores. At the end of Anna's party, you can buy a personalized DVD or link for downloading all the competitions and party events. Please stop by our Garoo Gift Shop on your way out to buy all things Kangaroo."

Anna finished picking the teams and everyone put on their shirts. Lacey heard Jimmy's annoying whiny voice rise above the group. She looked over at Maxwell and made her worst scrunchy face as if to say, "Ruh-roh, Rimmy".

Dark short hair and thick glasses sat atop an orange tent. Little Cousin Jimmy squeaked. "This shirt is too big for me! How am I supposed to win?"

He was small like his cousin Anna. His black eyeglasses were attached to the back of his head with an athletic safety strap. Jimmy's Flying Squirrel shirt was way too big and hung down to his knees. The armpits of the short-sleeved shirt sagged to his belly button area. The orange squirrel flapped his arms up and down like he was trying to gain flight.

Lacey stifled a giggle.

I know Anna gave him the biggest shirt on purpose.

Mr. Wild Roo said, "Mate step over here when we're done speaking, and I'll safety pin it to fit better."

Jimmy started to protest, but the boy returned to giving his speech. "Speaking of winning, you can follow which team is leading on our real-time scoreboards on the walls. Our next team matchup is the glow-in-the-dark rock wall. The Wall of Roos requires that each team member climb the rock wall and push the buzzer at the top to get a point. You'll be wearing safety ropes and helmets in case you fall, so again; no worries, birthday-goers. Keep in mind, if you do fall, you're out. No chance to try again."

Miss. Wild Roo gave instructions for the last game, TargetRoo. "You will each get a round glow target to wear around your neck as you enter Jumping Jacks Outback Village. You will also receive a boomerang laser popper. To hit a person's target, you point the boomerang directly at them. You have to be within range and then, ZAP, they're done!"

Everyone laughed and one kid shouted, "Zap!"

"Your target will vibrate and blink three times and turn off. This means you've received a fatal blow and you're out. Proceed to the exit to wait for the end of the game. While you're waiting, you can watch the remaining players on the TV screen. There is only one survivor at the end in TargetRoo. That team will win. Does anyone have questions?"

Out in the parking lot, the newly-released Wigglesworth had lots of questions as she sat in her car watching the front door to Wild Kangaroo Land Trampoline Park. Question number one. "Where is Lacey?" A simple google search of Lacey Honeycut revealed a recent post on Anna Chuong's Instagram. Anna shared a list of her friends attending today's birthday party which lead Mrs. Wigglesworth to this spot. She stared at her mugshot on her cell phone while she pondered question number two. "What am I going to do now?"

32

GLOWING CONTESTANTS

Lacey looked around the room to see who else was on her team and spotted Maxwell.

He's wearing an orange Flying Squirrels shirt. We're on different teams.

Anna ran up and gave her a hug. "Bestie, our Leaping Lizards will kick some squirrel butt today!"

Mr. Roo said, "Teams, follow us to the Zippyroo course."

Maxwell passed the girls and said, "Are you girls ready to rumble?"

Lacey stuck her tongue out at him and birthday girl said, "You're the one who should be ready!"

Orange squirrels and bright neon-green lizards lined up to get their helmets on and enter the Zippyroo sportsplex.

This place is mind-boggling!

A glowing zip line weaved a path through the room high above long trampolines. Painted glow-in-the-dark scenery decorated all the walls with anything that could jump, fly, or swing. The walls were covered with images of kangaroos jumping with baby-roos in their pouches. Squirrels hung from trapeze swings while frogs sat on their heads. Different colored monkeys climbed rock walls.

Everything is glowing. Lacey looked down at her shirt. *Even me.*

The Wild Roos arranged the contestants in one line with every other person on a different team. Jimmy was last in line wearing his recently safety-pinned orange shirt-dress and helmet. With a two-minute space between players, they started the game. The song by Tom Petty, "Free Falling," blared on the surround-sound speakers.

This will be an adrenaline rush of the best kind. After my late-night Dr. Lacey practice, I need a boost!

Her skinned knees ached as she climbed the zip line ladder. Anna took off ahead of her, gliding and laughing. The birthday Roo picked her target and let go.

My turn!

Lacey gripped the handle and lifted her feet off the platform. Instantly, she was zooming past bright lights.

I'm flying!

She raced above large and small targets.

Forget my skinned knees. I'm soaring like an eagle!!! I don't want this to end!

Lacey caught sight of the finish line. She let go, plummeting straight for the glow-in-the-dark purple target.

Boing, boing.

She hit the center of the target and immediately took a rebound bounce back up. She couldn't stop laughing.

I want to do that about five hundred more times!!

GLOWING CONTESTANTS

Lacey made her way toward the main area. She hoped that everyone on her team hit a target. The TV flashed the scores, as the last person zipped by. Everyone gathered around watching the screen. The score was 10–9. Lacey's Leaping Lizards had a perfect score!

All eyes looked at the big glowing orange shirt floating down the course. Jimmy held on tight to the end where he was introduced to the bouncy ball pool.

My team is ahead! Leaping Lizards 10, Flying Squirrels 9.

Jimmy climbed out of the bouncy pool with his head hanging low. Even Lacey felt bad for him.

"Blokes and Sheilas, hop on over to the climbing wall for the Wall of Roos contest.", announced a booming Roo voice.

At the climbing wall, Lacey and Anna sang along to *Ain't No Mountain High Enough.*

Lacey strapped her safety helmet back on and gave Anna a high-five. "We got this Birthday Roo!"

She clipped the safety rope onto her belt.

Okay, Lacey, deep breath. If I fall, I'll dangle on the safety swing until a staff member unhooks me. But I'm NOT going to fall!

She was at the back of the pack again. Climbers were going up in groups of four so the competition would go quickly with only twenty kids. Lacey gripped the rocks above her and climbed up placing her feet on the glowing rocks.

"Eeeeeek! Eeeeeek!" A baby wombat popped out right where she was about to grip the rock.

Lacey jerked her hand away and held on with her other hand.

"What the? What the wombat?"

The mechanical wacky wombat ducked back inside its hole. Lacey grabbed the rock and regained her stability.

Thanks for the warning, Roos.

Two more Australian critters popped out to scare her as she continued to clamber up, but this time, she was ready. As she climbed higher, Maxwell passed.

He shouted out, "See you at the bottom, lizard lips."

Lacey almost slipped again when he said lizard lips.

No way I will let Maxwell break my concentration.

A few minutes later, she caught up with him. Maxwell stopped climbing because Jimmy was above him blocking his way.

Jimmy sobbed loudly. "I can't do it. I will fall!"

As Lacey passed them, Maxwell shouted up to Jimmy. "Yes,

you can! We need your point! You're almost at the buzzer."

Jimmy kept blubbering. "I'm going to fa-fall. My shirt is too big."

Lacey reached for the buzzer.

Buzz!

She slowly started backing down the same way she had climbed up. Once again, she passed Jimmy and Maxwell.

Seriously?

Lacey couldn't believe her eyes. Jimmy stood on Maxwell's shoulders. Maxwell's face was bright red from exertion. He pushed Jimmy up the final step so he could reach the buzzer.

Buzz! Jimmy hit the buzzer.

Maxwell grunted at him and said, "Jimmy, you did it! Now get your feet off me and move out of the way so I can hit the buzzer. Whatever you do, don't fall off now. Just back down slowly."

Everyone was back at the bottom and gathered around to check the score. Leaping Lizards 20, Flying Squirrels 19. Nobody fell, which meant the Squirrels were still one point behind.

A boy named Thomas complained to the Wild Roos staff member. "Maxwell and Jimmy cheated."

Maxwell walked up and joined in the conversation, debating that there were no stated rules against lifting a team member up.

The Wild Roos put their heads together, intensely discussing the situation. Jimmy walked up and stood by the group. The staff leaders held up their hands to the crowd.

Ms. Roo said, "Blokes and Sheilas, after much discussion, we rule that the point counts."

A cheer rose up from the Flying Squirrels. They were still one point behind, but they had a chance to catch up now.

Maxwell clapped Jimmy on the back. "You did it!"

Jimmy grinned. Everyone made their way over to the final challenge at Jumping Jacks Outback Village.

Outside in the parking lot, two Smiths pulled drove up in a black, four-door car with tinted windows.

Agent Smith pointed at Mrs. Wigglesworth's car. "There she is. I'm sorry we lost her earlier, but I told you she'd be here."

"Park behind that van so she doesn't see us. How did you know she'd be here?"

"Wherever Lacey Honeycut goes, Wigglesworth follows."

33

TWERP WARS

At the entrance to Jumping Jacks Outback Village, the contestants traded their helmets for cool laser target necklaces and boomerangs. The song *I Get Knocked Down* by Chumbawamba was thump-thump-thumping at an earsplitting volume. Lacey stood next to Anna as they waited for the red traffic light to turn green.

She shouted, "Okay, birthday girl, we've got to hold on to our winning edge in this final competition. I suggest we stick together. I can cover in front of us and you watch behind us."

Anna shrugged and yelled back, "Sounds like a plan to me."

The light turned green and all twenty kids ran screaming into the village to take their places and wait for the starting siren. Lacey and Anna decided they would perch high on a bridge that had a good view of everything. The siren sounded, and the battle began. Kids were running everywhere, ducking and taking aim at each other. Lacey and Anna stayed in position as a battle strategy.

Maxwell ran by below, aiming at a girl with a green shirt and shrieking, "You're dead! You're dead meat!".

As they watched from above, shots were fired and dead players grudgingly made their way toward the exit. About fifteen minutes passed. It got very quiet. They didn't see any other kids.

Anna whispered, "I think they're all dead. It's over. We won!"

Lacey had to admit that it seemed like a good observation. However, in the back of her mind, she thought she remembered that a siren was supposed to go off when the game was officially ruled over.

She whispered, "I didn't hear the ending siren."

Anna stood up and held her hand out to help Lacey up. In a loud voice she said, "Come on partner, we're the last survivors."

Just as Lacey was about to take her hand, a small figure appeared directly below them, pointing a boomerang at Anna. Before Lacey could warn her, the shot was fired. Anna's necklace lit up, vibrated, then turned off. She stood frozen in complete shock. Without thinking, Lacey leaped up and tried to help Anna. That's when the figure from below fired again. Instantly. Lacey's target lit up, vibrated, and turned off. And just like that, the dynamic duo was dead.

Sirens sounded all around them, signaling the game was over. As the lights all came on, Lacey and Anna saw who delivered the fatal winning shots. Standing below them on the footpath with a huge grin on his face was little Cousin Jimmy.

Anna muttered, "Shot down dead by a TWERP!

All the guests from Anna's birthday party gathered at the Jumping Jukebox Café. The scoreboard on the wall read Leaping Lizards 29, Flying Squirrels 29. The teams were tied! Kids bunched in small groups talking and laughing. They relived the battle moves and everyone talked about Jimmy's final double kill.

Someone clever shouted, "Coming soon to a theater near you, *Jimmy 2, the Sequel—Revenge of the Cousin.*" Everyone laughed. Everyone except Birthday Roo.

The Wild Roos came to address the party. Mr. Wild Roo said, "Okay, settle down Mates. Crikey! This is a very rare occurrence at Wild Kangaroo Land. We have a deadlock. In the event of a tie-breaker, the Roo Rules are clear. The tie-breaker is a race to the finish line at the go-kart Roo Race track. The birthday-Sheila, Anna, will represent her Leaping Lizards team. She will compete with the Target Roo victor from the Flying Squirrels, Jimmy. Whoever wins this race wins the entire championship for their team."

Anna stood next to Maxwell and Lacey. She looked at them and reluctantly removed her beloved birthday tiara. She Handed it to Lacey. "Hold this for me. I will take Jimmy down because if I don't, my family will never let me forget it! Also, in case anyone is unclear, it's MY birthday!"

Cousins Anna and Jimmy sat side by side in racing go-karts, wearing helmets with their motors running. As they waited for the traffic light to turn green, a crowd gathered around the Roo Race track. People from everywhere at the trampoline park heard about the tie and were coming to watch the deciding race. Anna and Jimmy's family were watching as well as a few parents who arrived early for pickups.

The light turned green. Both drivers took off. Jimmy had a slight lead as he made the first turn. Anna gunned her go-kart, pushing the pedal all the way to the floor. She passed Jimmy but lost control of her kart in the turn because she was going so fast. She hit the brakes hard. Anna's kart slid into the bumpers and then bounced back into her lane. She was still in the lead.

They were coming up on the final stretch. It was a straight course to the finish line. Jimmy approached on her left. He was gaining speed on her.

Anna shouted through the gap in her helmet. "Not this time, little cousin. I'M the birthday Queen!"

For a second time, Anna gunned the foot pedal and held on tight to the wheel. She steered straight toward the finish line.

As her car inched in front of his, she yelled out, "Eat my dust, Twerp-boy!"

Jimmy couldn't catch her. Anna crossed the finish line first. "Winner" flashed in her lane. She waited for her kart to stop and hopped out. With both hands high in the air, she jumped up and down like a NASCAR champion. The Leaping Lizards rushed onto the track to celebrate with her. They were high fiving and hugging each other. Anna pulled off her racing helmet and broke into a rapcheer.

"Who's the top banana? Roo-Anna!

Who got first place? Birthday-Face!

Anna's the fastest racer. All you can do is chase-er.

Your team cries boo-hoo. Our team shouts Roo-Roo!"

Lacey was right there rejoicing with her team when she saw Jimmy getting out of his go-kart looking pitiful. He was holding his race helmet in one hand and looked like he was going to cry again. Anna's rhyming wasn't helping him man-up after the loss. Lacey decided for Jimmy's sake she'd better cut Anna off from her runaway rhyming train. Otherwise, the girl would go on forever!

Lacey grabbed Anna's hand and said, "Come on, Birthday-Roo, it's time for cake, ice cream, and PRESENTS!"

Lacey led Anna off the track and their team followed. Lacey looked back over her shoulder. Jimmy stood all alone on the track. His losing team had already moved on to the party room. Maxwell walked up to Jimmy and clapped him on the back. Maxwell said something to Jimmy, but Lacey couldn't hear what he said. Jimmy wiped his eyes with his sleeve and started to laugh. He gave Maxwell a high five, and they both walked toward the Jumping Jukebox Cafe.

By now, all the kids were ravenous. They ate pizza while Anna opened her presents. Anna's mom and dad brought out her pink kangaroo birthday cake. With her birthday tiara back in its rightful place, she blew out the candles while everyone sang *Happy Birthday*.

Wild Roos guy said, "Attention Blokes and Sheilas, thank you for celebrating Anna's birthday with us today. Crikey! That was a close race! You all must be knackered! Congratulations to team Leaping Lizards for your well-fought win. You can pick up your prize on the way out at the Garoo Gift Shop."

"Woo-Hooh!" The Leaping Lizards celebrated. "Lizards Rule! Lizards Rule!"

Ms. Wild Roo shouted above the chanting. "Remember, you can purchase a DVD of Anna's birthday party at our shop. And Flying Squirrels, you're not going home empty-handed. You put up an admirable fight. Your second-place prize can also be picked up at the Garoo Gift Shop."

The Flying Squirrels shouted and whistled, waving their arms in the air. "Squirrels! Squirrels! Squirrels!"

The birthday crowd made their way out. Lacey, Maxwell, and Anna stayed behind to help Anna's family pack up her presents and the leftover cake. It had been an amazing day. They were all tired, also known as knackered down under.

Lacey said to Anna, "That was the BEST birthday party I've ever been to! Sorry, I didn't bring your present, but I can give it to you tomorrow."

Anna teased, "Did you forget to buy me a present?"

Lacey said, "I was on my way to buy your present when something terrible happened."

Lacey told Maxwell and Anna the whole story about Tuffy.

Maxwell gave a low whistle. "You really assisted in surgery?"

Anna said, "Dr. Lacey Honeycut."

Lacey said, "It was scary and amazing. I'm so glad that Tuffy will be okay. Speaking of someone being okay. Maxwell, what did you say to Jimmy when he lost the race to keep him from crying?"

Maxwell shrugged. A wave of pink blush rose to cover his freckles. He said, "Oh Jimmy's not such a bad kid. He just needs more confidence and friends. I told him, you're a great cousin to let Anna-banana win that race."

Lacey, Anna, and Maxwell walked out the door. Wilma Wigglesworth ducked down behind the steering wheel.

34

BOOGER SOLUTIONS

The next morning, Lacey radioed Maxwell on the walky to remind him of their appointment at Booger's house.

Maxwell said, "I'll bring the Better Booger Prototype."

When Lacey rolled into Booger's driveway, Maxwell sat waiting in his mom's car.

Lacey walked up to the driver's window. "Good morning, Mrs. Ayce, are you helping us too?"

Maxwell's mom had on professor clothes. She looked too professional for walking dogs. Professor Ayce taught Ancient Civilizations and Linguistics at Meriwether Community College.

"Hi Lacey, I'm on my way to teach. Maxwell asked me to help deliver his prototype."

Maxwell got out of the car.

His mom asked him, "Do you need any help to lift it out of the trunk?"

"No, that's okay. It's not heavy. I designed it to fold up." He unloaded the prototype from the trunk. "Okay, thanks, Mom!"

"Have fun!" She waved and drove away.

Lacey stepped closer as Maxwell unfolded his invention. "Lacey, feast your eyes on the Booger Buggy prototype."

Lacey studied the Booger Buggy. It resembled a baby stroller except it was shorter and smaller. The top part was navy blue cloth with a net canopy that could pull forward and zip closed. The four wheels were oversized with bright yellow springy shocks. Each side of the buggy had solitary metal rings with hooks.

Maxwell pointed out the custom features. "I added the hooks so you can attach Stella to one side and Brutus to the other while Booger rides comfortably in his buggy. You can pull the shade forward to protect him from getting sunburned. You can zip the netting so he doesn't fall out. For added security, you can attach his harness to the ring on the inside of the buggy."

"Maxwell, you thought of everything!"

"There's more. I replaced the tires and changed the shocks for efficiency when traversing speed bumps or potholes. That's the practical reason for the big tires and bright yellow shock absorbers. The impractical reason is that it was a total blast designing the Booger Buggy to look like a hot rod baby carriage."

Lacey grabbed the handle and pushed the buggy around the circular drive, running at top speed. "Maxwell, I love it! Let's give it a test run!"

They parked the buggy out front. Maxwell went into the house to help Lacey get the dogs. Maxwell liked animals, but he wasn't a pet person. At the top of the stairs, he paused and eyeballed the gargantuan portrait of the dogs and their owner. "Interesting."

He followed Lacey to the dog room. Once he recovered from the shock of seeing hairless dogs dancing on their hind legs and wearing t-shirts; he helped Lacey with their harnesses and leashes. That is to say, he did the best he could to help Lacey. He had no idea how to catch the bopping canines. They were moving targets.

Lacey watched Maxwell's attempt at wrangling the rascals and laughed.

"Maxwell, I'll get them harnessed up and you can hold their leashes."

Downstairs, Lacey sprayed sunscreen on the dogs. Maxwell attached Stella's leash on one side and Brutus on the other side. Lacey lifted Booger and held him up to face her. He was wearing a black crystal-studded t-shirt that said "Boneland Security". Maxwell spied the shirt at the same time and they both laughed.

Lacey said softly to Booger, "Don't be afraid. I'm going to take you out in your Booger Buggy that Maxwell designed just for you."

She placed him in the stroller and pulled the sunshade closed to keep him from getting sunburned. Maxwell showed her how to attach his harness to the inside ring. Stella and Brutus were tugging on both sides like horses pulling a chariot and barking 'We're ready to rumble'

Maxwell walked with Lacey to monitor the test run. It was a quiet morning in Booger's neighborhood. After two circles around the block, Lacey held up her hand. "High five, Booger Buggy–builder!"

Maxwell met the slap up-high. "That's how I roll."

Maxwell peeked in the stroller to check on Booger. He was peacefully riding along taking in the view. "The test subject looks happy."

"Thanks to you! No more tangled leashes or pitiful shaking and whining. I've got three happy campers."

"Correction, four happy campers including you."

"Now our walks will seem like a walk in the park." Lacey chuckled at her humorous pun and stopped the buggy to take Booger out. She lifted him out and let him walk around in the empty grass field next to the tennis courts.

Booger finished his business. Lacey returned him to the Booger buggy and clipped him in. She left the netting open. "Here you go Booger. Now you'll have a nice view on the walk home. Lacey looked up and was caught by surprise. Mrs. Wigglesworth was approaching.

"What's SHE doing here?"

35

FLYING CURLERS

After spying on Lacey at the birthday party, Mrs. Wigglesworth calmed down. She got a good night's sleep, made a cup of tea, and put her curlers on. Her morning was going fine until she accidentally locked herself out of her house while retrieving the morning paper. She NEVER went out in public with curlers. Now she was locked out of her house in broad daylight where anyone of significance—or insignificance might spot her wearing curlers. Mrs. Wigglesworth mumbled to herself. She often mumbled to herself when she was agitated. Mrs. Wigglesworth was highly agitated.

As she hurried toward her neighbor's house, she mumbled, "First a mug shot, now curlers in public. Mother Wahnita must be flipping in her grave—flipping in her grave and disowning me. Stupid keys! Stupid mailbox! Stupid curlers! Stupid! Stupid! Stupid! Thank goodness I wasn't stupid when I hid a spare key in my neighbor's yard. I always knew the spare key hide-a-rock that I bought on eBay would save me from a stupid, stupid lockout. I'll just go a few houses down and get back inside before anyone sees me."

Lacey stood next to Maxwell and the Booger Buggy dreading Wilma's arrival. Mrs. Wigglesworth had large curlers in her hair, covered partially with a polka-dotted scarf. She was muttering something to herself and didn't see the pair until she almost ran into them. Startled, she saw Lacey and anxiously touched her hand to her head.

She frowned at the stroller and said, "I don't think it's appropriate for you to take care of children?"

Before Lacey or Maxwell could say anything, Mrs. Wigglesworth leaned her head into the stroller. Instead of a cute little baby, she came face to face with a BOOGER.

Mrs. Wigglesworth let out a loud yelp of surprise!

Booger let out a loud yelp of surprise!

Brutus and Stella joined in and let out multiple yelps of surprise!

In her rush to step back from the stroller and the weird baby inside it, her top curlers got caught in Booger's sunshade. She batted frantically with both hands, attempting to untangle her head from the shade. In the midst of the Curlers vs Booger Buggy wrestling match, one of her large plastic curlers went soaring into the air.

Mrs. Wigglesworth watched the airborne curler.

Maxwell and Lacey watched the airborne curler.

Mrs. Wigglesworth stood spellbound with a stunned expression plastered on her face.

One lonely unwrapped straggle of her gray hair flapped madly in the breeze.

Mrs. Wigglesworth scowled at Maxwell and Lacey.

Maxwell and Lacey scowled at Mrs. Wigglesworth.

Wigglesworth's wild flap of hair broke her eye contact, and she looked away.

Lacey and Maxwell continued to scowl at her.

Without bothering to retrieve her runaway curler, she half-jogged, half-sprinted back toward her house.

Maxwell looked at Lacey.

Lacey looked at Maxwell.

Maxwell started laughing first. He covered his mouth, attempting to stifle his uncontrollable laughter. Lacey joined in, chuckling gleefully.

Maxwell said, "That was priceless!"

"That's what she gets for picking on me."

"Once she recovers from her initial shock, I can just imagine how quickly her story will turn into Meriwether Pines news, 'Baby Space Alien Discovered in Lacey Honeycut's Stroller!'"

"He does kind of look like a space alien—a really ugly, really cute space alien."

Lacey looked up from Booger. Two girls were coming up the intersecting road pushing a baby stroller. Lacey pointed across the street. "Hey Maxwell, it's V-squared!"

"Valencia! Vanessa! Over here!"

They waved and came over. Stella and Brutus had recovered from Wigglesworth shock. They jumped and strained on their leashes attempting to say, 'Hello, aren't we adorable?'

Valencia exclaimed, "What? Dogs without fur?"

Lacey said, "Meet Stella and Brutus. They're Chinese Crested hairless dogs. I'm taking care of them while Charlotte is away. Don't worry, they're friendly."

Valencia kneeled down to pet Brutus. "Are you babysitting too?"

Lacey and Maxwell laughed.

Lacey replied, "The third dog is in the carriage. He doesn't get around too well, so Maxwell invented this cool buggy for him. Valencia and Vanessa, I'd like you to meet Booger."

Valencia and Vanessa said, "Booger!" at the same time (which twins often do—and not just the word 'booger', but lots of things).

They both peeked inside to see what a Booger looked like.

Vanessa said, "He's so cute and little. I thought you were pushing a baby around."

Maxwell said, "So did Mrs. Wigglesworth."

Vanessa said, "What's a Wigglesworth?"

Lacey said, "A troublemaker who got a big surprise when she

assumed Booger was a baby! Let's say she didn't handle the shock of a Boogerbabe too well. She ran off that way." She pointed up the street.

Maxwell walked over to check out the real baby. He asked Valencia, "Who is this cute boy—umm, sorry, girl. I can't tell when they're babies unless they're wearing pink or blue."

Valencia giggled. "Yes, I know what you mean. This is my godmother's son, Nathan. Isn't he sooooo beautiful!"

Vanessa chimed in. "She's letting us babysit him today. He's adorable! I could just kiss his little pudgy cheeks all-day-long."

Lacey leaned in and looked at baby Nathan. He was younger than her brother Petey and so cute. He had hazel-green eyes and a thick layer of soft curly brown hair. "Awe! He's beautiful. I'd love to walk with you and catch up with what your summer has been like so far. Are you going to the Meriwether Fourth of July celebration?"

Vanessa said, "Yes, we'll be performing our baton twirling routine."

Maxwell said, "I will be performing with my hip hop dance team. I've programmed my drone-bot R3 to film the event for me that day."

Lacey said, "That is so cool, Maxwell. I definitely want to watch the video afterward."

Maxwell said, "Lacey, I can take the dogs back if you want to catch up with Valencia and Vanessa."

"Would you? That would be great!"

Valencia said, "Thanks, Maxwell."

Vanessa said, "Yeah, thanks."

Maxwell took the Booger Buggy and guided Brutus and Stella back into position on each side. He said, "No problem. I wanted to take this for a spin myself, anyway. See ya later."

After Maxwell disappeared at the top of the hill, Lacey and Valencia stood next to the stroller, catching up.

Valencia said, "It's going to be such fun at the Fourth of July celebration. Our baton twirling dance team is called The Flaming Twirlettes."

Further up the street, Mrs. Wigglesworth stopped to catch her breath. "What was that THING in the stroller?"

36

ALIEN BABY

The second she saw its beady little eyes; Mrs. Wigglesworth switched into SURVIVAL mode. She was in a full panic. "I'm locked out of my house. I'm wandering the streets, with who knows what only blocks away from me! I need to get back into my house? Which authorities should I alert? Is this creepy creature connected to Lacey's criminal activities?"

A black Mercedes sedan slowed to a crawl and stopped next to her. The darkened driver's side window rolled down and a woman with a very concerned look on her face asked, "Mrs. Wigglesworth, is that you? Mrs. Wilma Wren Wigglesworth?"

Wilma looked at the woman, horrified as she realized who it was. Mrs. Betty Anne Ford, named after the late President Ford's late wife—and possibly a distant relative, sat in her Mercedes staring at Wilma. Mrs. Betty Anne Ford, President of the local chapter of The Society for Etiquette and Decorum was looking at her with CURLERS in her hair—well, most of them. Wilma's face turned redder than a traffic light, flashing stop! She stammered, "Hello Mrs. Ford—Mrs. Betty Anne Ford." Then for reasons only known to—no one, she performed some kind of awkward half curtsy.

Mrs. Ford replied, "My goodness, Mrs. Wigglesworth, are you okay?"

Mrs. Wigglesworth crossed over to the Mercedes and leaned her head close to the window for absolute privacy. She didn't want to lean her head all the way in fearing a second curler incident. In a low whisper she said, "Mrs. Betty Anne Ford—may I call you that?"

Mrs. Ford replied, "Of course."

"Mrs. Betty Anne Ford, I have something to share with you, and it is important that you remain calm. I've just come face to face with an ABERRATION. It's a completely different species, frightening and small."

Mrs. Betty Anne Ford was taken aback. "What do you mean?"

Before she could get a reply, Mrs. Wigglesworth scooted around the front of the Mercedes and jumped into the passenger seat. She pointed with a shaky finger and said, "It went that way!"

Mrs. Ford, sensing the sincere fear and urgency (and possible insanity) in Wilma's voice, drove as directed. As the black car approached, the girls were still engrossed in their discussion about the Fourth of July. Vanessa said, "Our baton twirling dance team is performing the same routine that won us the state championship."

Valencia said, "The choreography and music are a huge crowd-pleaser. We have a surprise in the routine that blows everyone's minds but I can't tell—"

A big black Mercedes stopped directly next to them. Out popped Mrs. Wigglesworth from the passenger seat. She was shouting something to the driver who opened the driver's side door. Mrs. Wigglesworth grabbed the woman's hand and pulled her over to the carriage, shouting, "Here it is! I told you! It's right inside there. That thing is alive. Make sure it's still there and we can use your cell phone to alert the authorities!"

Conversation stopped between the girls. The lady wearing a brown pantsuit said, "Hello, I'm so sorry to trouble you. My name is Mrs. Betty Anne Ford and Mrs. Wigglesworth has asked me to help her clear up a misunderstanding about—"

"—Oh, it's no misunderstanding. And THIS ONE," she pointed her trembling finger at Lacey. "Is clearly up to no good. Just lo-lo-lo-look in that carriage!"

Mrs. Ford, who was obviously uncomfortable, said to Lacey, "Do you mind if I take a quick peek in the carriage?"

Lacey pointed at the twins. "They're the babysitters. I'm sure they won't mind."

The confused twins rotated their heads in combined agreement and bewilderment. It was sort of a circular head motion conveying "yes" and "no" at the same time.

Mrs. Wigglesworth shouted, "Be careful, Betty! Be VERY careful!"

All eyes were on Mrs. Ford as she leaned into baby Nathan's carriage. An adorable green-eyed baby giggled and drooled, waving his pacifier around. She looked at Mrs. Wigglesworth, motioning for her to step forward. "THIS is what frightened you?"

Mrs. Wigglesworth inched up to the stroller and cautiously leaned in to see baby Nathan. She felt faint. All the oxygen seemed to be exiting her brain. When baby Nathan saw her head with curlers, he started happily gurgling and clapping his little pudgy hands together.

Lacey thought, *that baby really likes curlers.*

Without a word, Mrs. Wigglesworth turned and mechanically

walked back to the car. She opened the passenger door and got in.

Mrs. Ford looked at the girls and said politely, "I apologize profusely for this unfortunate encounter. I will drive Mrs. Wigglesworth home where I am sure she will have a cup of tea and take a long warm bath followed by a much-needed nap." She got back into her car and said something to Mrs. Wigglesworth that was muffled by the closing door. Then they drove away.

It took quite some time for Lacey to explain the entire story to Valencia and Vanessa. She ended it with, "Can you believe all her warped and wonky WACUSATIONS?"

Vanessa said, "Wow! Lacey, she's been causing you so much trouble!

Valencia said, "This is seriously messed up!"

Back in the Mercedes, Mrs. Wigglesworth was seriously messed up. She was shaking and embarrassed. She directed Mrs. Ford to the hide-a-key location and retrieved her spare key. They pulled into her driveway.

Always the picture of etiquette, Mrs. Ford said, "Mrs. Wigglesworth, it was so lovely to see you again. We should get together sometime for tea and biscuits."

Mrs. Wigglesworth mumbled, "Yes, thank you," and got out of the car.

Mrs. Ford pulled out and drove up the street a few blocks. She pulled her car over and dialed a number on her car phone. A young woman answered. "Hello, Women's Society for Mental Health and Midlife Crisis Intervention, how may I help you?"

Mrs. Ford said, "I need to file a report about Mrs. Wilma Wren Wigglesworth."

37

MINUSCULE VISITOR

Lacey woke up, stretched, and yawned. Drowsy woke up, stretched, and yawned.

It's the Fourth of July! I will not think about Wigglesworth. It's time for family, friends, fun, and fireworks!

Lacey jumped out of bed. Drowsy did not jump out of bed. She gave one of her drawn-out meyawns, rolled onto Lacey's pillow, and went back to sleep. *That cat! What a life!*

Lacey and her favorite Scooby-Doo slippers skipped over to her music player. *Born in the USA* by Bruce Springsteen shook the speakers. She loved to rock out to this song. Usually, she would pick Drowsy up (or any available pet) and dance around the room. The sleeping Drowsy was definitely not up for dancing right now and Mickey was not around. He must have gotten up early or stayed up all night.

He is nocturnal.

Lacey put on her favorite faded jean shorts, red-and-white-striped tank top, and a blue baseball hat with a horse on it. She grabbed her blue and white-stars sneakers and strummed her air guitar. "Born in the USA!"

Statue of Lacerty

Lacey danced around her bedroom and sang along to the words. She stood her air guitar straight up and strummed the chorus.

Knock, knock

Lacey lowered the music and dropped her air guitar—sort of. She opened the door and there stood Grandpa Sam Sam. He hugged her tight then held her at arms-length to examine her. "Lacey, you've grown ten feet since the last time I saw you!"

"Grandpa Sam Sam, you know that's not possible. I'd be a giant."

Her grandpa had a silly smirk on his face. "There were giants in the bible times, maybe they're making a comeback." He eyeballed her entire outfit. "Somebody's ready to celebrate the birth of our country. Let's go downstairs and start with a hearty breakfast. I stopped at Dunkin Donuts on my drive-in."

Lacey grabbed her walky off the charger. "Grandpa Sam Sam. I definitely inherited my sweet tooth from you! Where's Grandma?"

Grandpa said, "She is in New York at some highfalutin' dog show. You know how she is with those big poodles of hers. I'm sure they'll come back home with more ribbons and tacky-looking poodley trophies. I'll have to build more shelves for in her trophy room. Did I tell you we have an entire dog brag room now in the house?"

Lacey said, "A whole room of trophies? That's impressive. You know I love animals just as much as Grandma." They walked into the kitchen and Lacey headed straight for the Dunkin Donuts box. Mickey was sprawled across the top of the box.

"There you are." She picked him up. "No donuts for you today."

Mickey complained, "*Hey! I was just keeping them safe from the cat. It's not like I was going to eat any. But now that you mention it, if you have a powdered cheese stuffed donut with chocolate sprinkles, I could take it off your hands.*"

Grandpa Sam Sam said, "Lacey, I didn't know you had a mouse. I've never seen one like that. He looks like someone sprayed him with shiny blue spray paint."

Lacey held Mickey close to her grandpa's face. "I know Grandpa. I rescued him from a terrible experimental laboratory in New York. I think he may have Argyrosis. It's a condition caused by exposure to chemical compounds with silver. It made him turn blue."

Mickey let out a high-pitched squeal so high that dogs in the neighborhood began to howl. *"Blue? What? BLUE! Soggy sailor, sarcastic Smurf teen and EVERYONE else was right? I'm BLUE?"* He jumped out of Lacey's hand and ran towards the downstairs guest bathroom screaming, *"I've got to find a mirror. Where is a mirror?"*

Grandpa Sam Sam laughed as they watched Mickey run off squealing loudly. He said, "Being blue hasn't slowed him down any."

Lacey had never heard Mickey squeal like that. She watched him race out of sight and shrugged her shoulders. She picked out two chocolate cream-filled donuts and poured a glass of orange juice. "Grandpa, aren't you having one?"

"No, it's bad for my cholesterol or something like that. I'm saving myself for the barbecue at the picnic today."

Lacey's walky beeped, and she heard Anna's voice. "Walky #2. This is walky #1 come in."

Lacey's grandpa raised his eyebrows at the walky-talky. She said, "I'll tell you all about it at the breakfast table. We have a lot to catch up on."

Mom and Steve, with Petey in tow, walked into the kitchen and said, "Good morning."

Lacey replied to Anna, "Walky #2 coming in. Happy Independence Day! Over."

Anna came back. "What's the plan, rubber band? Over."

"Let's meet at the funnel cake stand at noon. Over."

"Yum! See you at noon! Don't forget to wear red, white, and blue! Over."

Lacey shot back, "Dah! Over and out."

As everyone gathered at the table for a late breakfast, Lacey gave Grandpa Sam Sam the all-things-Lacey-update. Mom gave him the all-things-Petey-update. Grandpa Sam Sam was bouncing Petey on his lap while listening and making crazy, silly faces at him. He paused, mid-funny face. "Whoa, Nelly!" (This is an old-fashioned saying Lacey and her grandpa love that means hold your horses.) "You're telling me that Lacey is running a small business all by herself?"

Lacey proudly said, "You got it, Grandpa Sam Sam."

It was Lacy who named him *Grandpa Sam Sam* when she was little. After that, the name just stuck. He was so much fun to be around. When he was very young, he used to perform in vaudeville shows. He traveled from town to town, dancing, singing, and playing his harmonica.

Mom said, "Dad has a surprise for you. Dad, tell Lacey what you are doing at the Meriwether Pines town center."

Grandpa Sam Sam said, "Lacey, you know I still sing and play the harmonica. I'm in this barbershop quartet named Dapper Old Whippersnappers. We're performing today."

Lacey pumped her fist in the air. "Whoop-Whoop, Grandpa Sam Sam has Pappy Power! You're going to be on the same stage with three of my friends today. Maxwell is performing with his hip-hop group and the twins, Valencia and Vanessa, are in the show with their baton twirling."

Mom said, "Okay, gang, let's get these dishes cleaned and pack up. We need the picnic basket, cooler, all drinks and food, blankets, sparklers, and all Petey's baby stuff."

Everyone was ready to go. It looked like they packed for a week trip with all the Petey paraphernalia.

Geez, how much stuff does a baby need?
Ding dong.
Who is at the door?

38

BLUE SHOCK

A man stood on the front porch with a large bag on his shoulder. He had dark eyes framed by wire glasses and short dark hair. He wore a white button-down shirt with tan khaki pants. Lacey looked at a cloth sling crossed over the front of his shirt.

He said, "Are you Lacey?"

"Yes, I am."

The man held out his hand to shake. "I'm Dr. Sandeep Bhaiyyani. Charlotte's mother gave me your address. I hope you'll forgive me for intruding on your holiday. May I come in?"

Mom stepped forward. Lacey's whole family gathered behind her. The man stepped inside and shook hands with Mom and Steve. "Nice to meet you."

Lacey said, "Dr. Bay—Dr. Bay—Yanny—"

Dr. Sandeep Bhaiyyani helped Lacey out. "People call me Dr. B."

"Thanks. Dr. B, why did Charlotte's mother send you over? Is it Charlotte? Is she ill?"

Dr. B chuckled and shook his head. "No, I'm not that kind of doctor. As far as I know, Charlotte is doing just fine. I'm the one who needs your help. I am a DVM, Doctor of Veterinary Medicine. I serve as president of the APV, Association of Primate Veterinarians, specializing in studying and training primates. I phoned Charlotte's mother because Charlotte had occasionally walked my poodle Fi-Fi for me. That's when I learned that Charlotte is out of the country and you have taken over her animal business. I have a family emergency that requires me to fly out of town immediately. I will be back by tomorrow. I really apologize for the—"

Mom interrupted. "Don't worry, Dr. Bhaiyyani. I'm sure Lacey can fit in your poodle Fi-Fi today. We can drive her over to your house."

Dr. Bhaiyyani said, "Oh thank you, that is so kind of you, but Fi-Fi is staying at her groomer's house. She was already scheduled for grooming when this emergency came up."

"Dr. B, I'm confused. If you don't need help with Fi-Fi, why are you here?"

Dr. Bhaiyyani smiled a little sheepishly and opened the cloth flap hanging across his shirt. A tiny little monkey head popped up and looked at everyone. Dr. Bhaiyyani said, "I'm here because of Mr. Man."

The tiny monkey climbed out of the pouch and up to the doctor's neck. He clung to the collar of his shirt.

He's literally the most adorable monkey I've ever laid eyes on!

Mr. Man emitted small chortling sounds and made a funny face. He had on a tiny blue t-shirt, "Will Work for Bananas". He turned and looked at Lacey.

Stepdad Steve said, "What in the world is that?"

Dr. Bhaiyyani said, "Allow me to introduce Cebuella pygmaea, a pygmy marmoset. This is a small species of the New

World monkey native to rainforests of the western Amazon Basin in South America. The species is notable for being the smallest monkey and one of the smallest primates in the world, or better known to me as Mr. Man."

Lacey said, "Mr. Man, you are the cutest monkey I've ever seen."

Mr. Man blew her kisses. Everyone started laughing. Mr. Man jumped from Dr. Bhaiyyani to Lacey, landing on her shoulder.

Lacey took the tiny monkey in both of her hands. "You can blow me kisses anytime!"

Dr. Bhaiyyani said, "As you can see, he is extremely friendly. Socialization is an imperative building block for the study I am conducting. People shouldn't keep these primates as pets unless they are under the supervision of a professional. He lives at home with me and Fi-Fi. I train and socialize him as much as possible. He goes to work with me and out in public every day. Mr. Man has far exceeded my expectations. I carry him in this pouch I'm wearing."

Lacey said, "I was wondering what that was."

"When my family emergency came up this morning, I was in a complete conundrum. I can't take him on the plane with me. That's when I thought of Charlotte. I know this is a colossal inconvenience, but could you take care of Mr. Man today and keep him overnight? I will be back tomorrow afternoon."

Lacey exclaimed, "Monkey sitting! Are you kidding? Sign me up!"

Steve said, "Dr. Bhaiyyani, we're going to the Meriwether Pines Fourth of July celebration. We'll be there all day and stay for the fireworks tonight. What will Lacey have to do to take proper care of Mr. Man?"

At the mention of his name, Mr. Man, who was standing on Lacey's shoulder, looked at Steve and took a bow.

Everyone laughed.

This monkey is funny!

Dr. Bhaiyyani grinned. "I have trained him to take a bow when introduced by his name. His success rate is approximately forty-six-point eight percent."

Then to Steve, he said, "Thank you for that question. I assure you Mr. Man can go anywhere you are going. You will not need to alter your holiday plans. He has excellent manners and is being prepped as a candidate for space training at NASA."

This impressed Steve. "A space monkey? That's fascinating."

Stepdad and Mom exchanged looks and a small nod of agreement. Steve said to Dr. Bhaiyyani, "Okay, let's add a monkey to our troop."

Dr. Bhaiyyani made a small clap with his hands and said, "Excellent!"

He turned to Lacey and said, "Lacey, if you have a few minutes, I can sit down with you and go over his routines and needs. I see you have a baby brother. Just think of Mr. Man as another baby brother."

Mom laughed. "Dr. B. Now you're speaking my language."

Lacey cuddled Mr. Man. "Very funny, Mom. Mr. Man won't be any trouble. He'll probably add to the fun of the day and I promise to take care of him all by myself. Plus, Anna will be there today and she can help me."

As they headed out the door, Lacey shouted, "Bye Drowsy and Mickey!"

Mickey didn't hear her parting words. His ears were ringing like someone had boxed him in the head repeatedly. His head was spinning. He felt dizzy. His mouth couldn't do anything but gape open in shock. The rest of his body was limp and felt like it might float away or fall off the bathroom faucet. Mickey's eyes were working just fine. They focused in on the shiny BLUE mouse who was also standing on a bathroom faucet in the mirror looking back at him.

"*I'm REALLY BLUE! Now, what do I do?*"

39

HAT DANCING

Meriwether Pines celebrated the Fourth of July in a BIG way. The lineup for the day was an old-fashioned fair on the commons followed by a barbecue cook-off and family picnic time. Then at 3 p.m., people moved to the open-roof amphitheater with stadium seating. On stage, the mayor would be speaking, providing pompous and useless information in between performances. This year's show featured music by the Salvation Army and other entertainment. The final big event before the exciting Blue Angels flyover and fireworks was the annual hot dog eating contest.

The Hot Digitty Dawgalicious competition pitted last year's champion against this year's local winner. A panel of judges chosen from community leaders sat on the stage every year to observe the contest. In the event of a close call or dispute, they voted on the winner.

When Lacey's family and monkey arrived, there was already a nice crowd milling around the fair. The Oscar Mayer Wienermobile sat next to the main stage offering free hot dogs. Loudspeakers on the Wienermobile played the Perry Como song, "Hot Diggity." People were already claiming their turf with blankets, folding chairs, and coolers. Lacey's family left in search of the perfect spot to spread out and park the baby. Lacey went to meet Anna with Mr. Man strapped across her shirt. He was curled up in the pouch, sleeping.

Lacey spied Anna at the funnel cake stand and waved. Anna was wearing a red handkerchief sundress with blue-and-white sandals. Anna had a digital camera and a small camcorder strapped around her neck with a camera bag on her shoulder. "Hi Lacey, let's split a funnel cake and get this party started."

"Sounds good. Hey, why so many cameras?"

"I'm covering the entire event. Then I'll try to sell some pictures and maybe a story to the *Meriwether Tribune*." Anna pointed at Lacey's pouch., "Why the pouch? Are you continuing my birthday kangaroo theme?"

Lacey smirked. "Have I got a surprise for you! Get your cameras ready to take photos and videos of this."

Lacey opened the pouch. Mr. Man popped his head out and looked around. His nap was officially over.

Anna shrieked. "What is that?"

Mr. Man climbed out of the pouch, shimmied up Lacey's hair, and settled in on top of her baseball cap. "That," said Lacey, "is Mr. Man. I'm watching him until tomorrow."

At hearing his name, Mr. Man took several bows. Anna immediately grabbed her camera and started going crazy snapping pictures of Lacey with a monkey on her head. In between shots, she said, "I never knew a monkey could be so small! I want one—but no way, my parents would kill me."

Lacey said, "People call them pocket monkeys because they're so small. They don't make good pets because they have a lot of requirements. But today, I'm the luckiest girl in the world to have a monkey on my head."

They both broke into hysterics.

Mr. Man held his tiny belly and chuckled.

Anna said, "Monkey see, monkey do!"

Lacey tore the funnel cake in half and handed Anna a piece. "Hey, famous photographer, take a break and eat this while it's hot."

As the two best friends made their way to the Dunk the Clown booth, people everywhere pointed and stared at Mr. Man. His monkey manners were perfect until he spotted a clown wearing a big floppy flannel hat with sunflowers sticking out on top. He made a few clicking noises, let out a high-pitched screech, and vaulted onto the clown's hat. The clown thought this was hysterical and danced a little jig next to the dunking booth. The song *Gettin' Jiggy Wit It* by Will Smith was playing at the clown booth.

Anna pointed her camera.

Click, click.

Lacey said, "Anna, shoot some video for our Trias-Lab YouTube channel. Who can resist a monkey dancing on a clown's hat?"

Mr. Man chortled with glee and broke into a new dance move. *He's doing the Dougy!*

People gathered around and some kids started doing the Dougy too. Everyone standing nearby laughed and clapped, apparently thinking the monkey was part of the clown show.

Lacey took the dancing machine from the clown. "Thanks for playing along. This little dude is obsessed with hats."

The clown bowed several times and climbed back onto the dunking booth. Lacey settled the little rascal back on her hat and they walked on to the beanbag toss.

Anna said, "That's one talented monkey. He needs to go on that TV dancing show. I got some funny pictures of him and clowny-head. Did I tell you that my cousin Jimmy is in the hot dog eating contest? He's going against last year's champion."

"You're kidding! Why is it always the skinny kids who can eat so much?"

"I know! Skinny little cousin Jimmy."

After bean bag tossing, shoot the can, and a fortune-teller who was too distracted by Mr. Man to make any sense, Lacey said, "Hey, let's work our way back over to my family's camp spot. I'm ready for some barbecue and I need to feed monkey-face."

"Kewl with me. Where's Maxwell today? I thought he'd be here."

"He's performing with his hip-hop group. V-squared are twirling batons, and Grandpa Sam Sam is harmonizing."

Where's your arch enemy today?

40

SPY PLANS

Lacey said, "You mean Wigglesworth? Hopefully, nowhere near here."

Lacey's family had tons of food spread out when they got there. Petey's face was covered in barbecue sauce.

The boy knows how to wear food.

Anna gave her hellos to everyone and sat next to Lacey with a big plate of vegetarian food. Mom always made special menu choices for Anna. Lacey opened Mr. Man's bag and gave him some dried fruit to eat.

Mom said, "How's it going with the monkey?"

"So far, so good. He's got some dance moves. He's also obsessed with hats. He jumped up on my hat then made a huge scene when he jumped on a clown's hat."

Grandpa Sam Sam hee-hawed., "He was just clowning around."

Anna said, "I think he was monkeying around."

Grandpa Sam Sam and Anna laughed together at their amazing mutual cleverness.

Lacey rolled her eyes.

Ring-a-ling, ring-a-ling.

Mom grabbed her purse and pulled out her phone. She looked at the caller ID and answered the phone. "Hi, Bruce."

The voice on the phone said, "Hi Sara, I'm calling from Los Angeles. Happy Fourth of July! I was hoping to catch Lacey and chat with her for a few minutes. Is she around?"

"Perfect timing Bruce, she's right here." Mom held the phone out for her and said, "It's your dad."

Lacey grabbed the phone. "Hi, Daddy, Happy Independence Day! We're having a picnic at the town center. I'm having so much fun! We've been at the fair. We have tons of food and Grandpa Sam Sam is here. Guess what? I've got a mini-monkey with me!"

Dad said, "Hello Elfie! Happy Fourth! I'm so glad you're having fun! I am not at all surprised that you have a monkey with you! I'm sure he loves you because all animals are drawn to you."

Sometimes Dad says the sweetest things. "I wish you were here! Anna's here and a few of my friends will be in the show later."

Dad is a movie director in Hollywood. He said, "I'm sending you a big hug from beautiful, sunny California! I'm having dinner with your grandma and grandpa tonight and they asked me to send you good karma and joy." Lacey's other grandparents, Sunshine and Bud, lived in California and were hippie-cool people. "I don't want to interrupt your festivities. This is just a quick call to tell you I love you and I can't wait to see you when you visit for Christmas vacation!"

Lacey said, "It's going to be a blast! Two weeks in sunny-Cali with you!"

"I've got a big surprise for you when you visit. I can't tell you what it is. I'm directing a really cool sci-fi movie with lots of animals."

Lacey shouted, "What? Sci-fi animals? Tell me! I'm begging! Please, Daddy!"

"No way. That's why they call it a surprise. I'll tell you when it gets closer to your visit. I've got to run. Have fun today!"

"Come on, Dad, just one more teeny tiny hint!!!!"

"Tell me you love me and give the phone back to your mother."

"I love you and I'm giving the phone back to Mother."

She sat next to Anna. "That was my dad. He has some kind of animal movie sci-fi surprise for me when I visit him for Christmas Vacation."

Anna said, "I love science fiction movies."

Lacey and Anna stuffed themselves with so much food that they could barely move. Lying on the blanket next to each other, they stared at the sunny, cloudless sky. Lacey spied R3 hovering above them. She pointed to Maxwell's weird insect-bot. "Anna, there's R3, he's filming the event."

They watched as R3 flew toward the stage and out of sight. Mr. Man was snoozing in his pouch. The sky was crystal blue. It was a perfect day to share with her best girlfriend.

Anna said, "Let's have a bestie day tomorrow. We can go to the mall and spend some of my birthday money. Then we can catch a movie. My dad can drive us."

"Actually, Anna, I had something else in mind."

"What?"

"We're using Mickey to spy on Wigglesworth's house."

41

FLAMING GIRLS

After helping pack everything back into the car, they all headed to the amphitheater. Mom wanted to sit close to the back, near the bathroom in case Petey had issues. Lacey and Anna needed to sit up front to see the performances and capture better photographs for Anna. They agreed to meet after the show and found seats in the very first row.

Just as they settled in their seats, the Salvation Army band marched onto the stage playing *God Bless America*. They filed behind the podium and the mayor of Meriwether Pines came out. He asked the crowd to stand and led them in the Pledge of Allegiance. A gaggle of Brownies and Cub Scouts sang *This Land is Your Land* and played triangles, tambourines, and sticks. Anna stood up snapping videos and still shots of it all. Mr. Man was in his pouch.

He's not impressed.

More boring windbag words from the mayor and then it was Grandpa Sam Sam time! He was dapper in his red-and-white striped shirt with blue stars suspenders. He had on a straw hat and an American flag bow tie. The Dapper Old Whippersnappers were a crowd favorite when they harmonized to, *You're a Grand Old Flag* followed by a Pentatonix version of *My Country Tis of Thee.* They were so popular that they did an encore round-robin of *A Bicycle Built for Two, Daisy Daisy.*

Maxwell's hip hop team flipped and slid onto the stage as the Whippersnappers exited.

The Kool Moves wore baggy red pants, blue-and-white shirts, and sported long gray Uncle Sam beards on their faces. Lacey almost fell out of her chair laughing. A *Yankee Doodle Dandy* techno remix was boom-boom-booming as they moonwalked, side-kicked, and landed in full splits.

How are they keeping their tall Uncle Sam hats and their beards from falling off?

Maxwell took the lead and did a solo dance to *R.O.C.K. in the USA*.

The boy has moves!

Maxwell spotted Lacey and Anna and delivered a wink.

Lacey yelled, "Zoinks! That was amazing!"

Mr. Man snoozed on through the act. As the song faded out, Katy Perry's *Firework* started. The lyrics were about letting your light shine. Kool Moves took their cue, cartwheeling and flipping off the stage. The Flaming Twirlettes marched onto the stage, dressed from head to toe in white.

They look like snow princesses.

They sported tall white boots, sparkling white bejeweled leotards, and short white gloves. All the girls had their hair up in high ponytails tied with American flag bows. Their baton twirling and high throws were synchronized perfectly to the music. Suddenly the stage went completely dark and the lyrics of Alicia Keys, *Girl on Fire* penetrated the darkness. A small flame lit the darkness, then another and then many. Boom!

Spinning flames ignited. The flames burned and soared on their own until tiny flickering lights on each girl's leotard lit up, revealing the baton-twirling team. They tossed their blazing batons high in the air, catching and twirling them with amazing speed and agility. Vanessa and Valencia smiled widely through the entire song, concentrating on the routine, now complicated by fire. The Flaming Twirlettes had a flawless performance. They marched off the stage to Alicia Keys' words about a girl on fire.

The crowd went crazy. Everyone was giving a standing ovation. The lights came back on the stage and the mayor walked out to the podium. He was still clapping. He addressed the electrified group. "Meriwether Pines, do we have a talented town?"

42

DIGITTY DAWGALICIOUS

The crowd shouted, "Yes!"

Mr. Man finally woke up and poked his little head out of the pouch to see what all the shouting was about. Lacey gave him some water and a snack. He climbed on top of her hat to eat his snack and take in the show.

Lacey thought, "His own personal movie theater is on my head."

The mayor said, "I extend my undying gratitude to all the hard-working citizens behind the scenes and on the stage, who have made this Fourth of July one to remember. Don't go anywhere. We're just getting started. We still have the Blue Angels flyover and the famous Meriwether Pines fireworks extravaganza—graciously paid for by you, the taxpayers. And now without further ado, the event you've all been waiting for. It's time for the annual Hot Digitty Dawgalicious competition."

The crowd started clapping.

Mr. Man started clapping.

Everyone around Lacey pointed and laughed at the clapping monkey on her head.

Click, click.

Lacey grinned.

This just gets better and better. A cheering monkey on my head. How lucky could one girl get?

Behind the mayor's podium, the stage was getting set for the hot dog contest. They put tables and rolling bins of hot dogs in place.

The mayor said, "Before we get started, I want to introduce our distinguished panel of judges. In the event of a tie or dispute, they will decide the winner." As he spoke, they moved a table directly to the front of the stage next to Lacey and Anna. They placed it sideways for a view of the mayor and the hot dog table. They draped it with a red, white, and blue table skirt that read *Hot Digitty Dawgalicious Judges*.

Mr. Man was still clapping and chirping out happy noises.

He must really love hot dogs.

The mayor continued, "Our first judge is someone you all know and love. Coach Vargas has led the Meriwether Pines Panthers football team to the State Championship SIX times! Please welcome Coach Vargas."

A tall and stout man wearing a t-shirt, shorts, and sneakers, with a whistle dangling from his neck, waved at the crowd and jogged to the judges' table. He took a seat in the closest chair to the hot dog venue. The crowd applauded and a few kids (probably Meriwether Pines Panthers) gave a "WHOO! WHOO! Vargas"!

The mayor carried on. "Next up we have a very important member of our community. Her roots in this town go back generations. Please give a warm welcome to Mrs. Betty Anne Ford, president of the local chapter of the Society for Etiquette and Decorum."

Mrs. Ford strode onto the stage to a pleasant round of applause.

It's Wigglesworth's friend from the Booger Buggy drama!

She was wearing a navy-blue pantsuit with a white starched shirt and a red carnation in the lapel of her jacket. Mrs. Ford smiled politely and gave a little wave to the crowd, then took her seat next to Coach Vargas.

The mayor glanced down at his notes and seemed flustered. He looked back at the audience. "I apologize. My assistant handed me this agenda before I came on stage. I was expecting to introduce the third judge who is a good friend of mine and much beloved in this town. He has come down with the flu and cannot attend.

"We have a last-minute addition to our distinguished panel of judges. I have never heard of her, but my paper says that she is the president of The Honorable Society to Empower Female Women Worldwide and Across the Universe." At reading this title, the mayor furrowed his eyebrows and looked confused. "Ladies and gentlemen, please give a warm welcome to a woman who was so gracious to join our panel of judges at the last minute, Mrs. Wilma Wren Wigglesworth."

Lacey and Anna gawked at each other in shock.

There was a smattering of clapping and Mrs. Wigglesworth paraded onto the stage. She was wearing a long red fitted skirt and jacket with a big-collared white blouse. A wide red ribbon was around her neck like a Victorian choker and tied in a bow at the back. But the thing that was most eye-popping was her hat."

I think I saw that hat on my field trip to the Victorian history museum.

The hat was tight on the top of her head and tied in the back with a huge red ribbon. The snug part created some sort of platform for the huge top, which looked like a pasture and garden growing on her head. It started high in the back and dipped out in front of her face dripping with ivy vines, flowers, and colorful dragonflies.

Newsflash! Crazy Wilma wearing a crazy hat!

Mrs. Wigglesworth strode in slightly sideways, facing the crowd as if in a beauty pageant, with both hands raised and waving. She took her place at the table next to Mrs. Betty Ford and closest to the crowd. She gave a small nod to Mrs. Ford then a large smile to the crowd.

I didn't think she knew how to smile.

The mayor, shocked and weirdly impressed by her bodacious hat vineyard, continued to speak. "Meriwether Pines, please welcome the Hot Digitty Dawgalicious reigning champion and a member of IFOCE, the International Federation of Competitive Eating, Becky-Hotdog-Danbury."

The crowd applauded as a tall and muscular girl with red hair walked over and stood behind the hot dog table. She was very pale and covered in tattoos. She wore plain black shorts and a plain black tank top.

The mayor said, "And now our underdog this year—" He chuckled into the microphone at his witty hot dog joke. He cleared his throat and said, "Let's meet Jimmy Tang, the winner of this year's county seat hot dog-eating contest."

People clapped as little Jimmy nervously walked behind the table and stood by Hotdog- Becky. He looked like an Oompa Loompa next to her. Lacey was half-expecting him to break out singing, "Oompa loompa do-ba-dee-da doompadeedoo."

Hot Digitty Monkeylicious

A dancing hot dog (or at least a person dressed like one), exited the Oscar Mayer Wienermobile and stepped on the stage. He danced over to the podium and did a jig around the judges' table. At the sight of the dancing hot dog, Mr. Man slid off Lacey's hat and down Lacey's neck, clinging to her shirt.

She comforted him and patted his head. "It's okay Mr. Man, it's just a dancing hot dog.".

The mayor said, "The Oscar Mayer Wienermobile and Mr. Wienerman have traveled all the way here from New York City. They are offering free hot dogs after the contest, and Mr. Wienerman will autograph photographs of himself."

Laughter broke out everywhere when Mr. Wienerman gave a

final salute, touched his forehead (insomuch as a hot dog has a forehead) and exited the stage.

Does little cousin Jimmy stand a chance of winning?

43

BAD MONKEY

Mr. Man, feeling safe again, climbed back up on Lacey's hat. He was facing the crowd with his back to the stage. Anna was standing next to Lacey. She snapped so many pictures and video footage that she had to change out both memory cards. As she made the switch, she said to Lacey, "I'm getting some great stuff! This has to make the local paper!"

The mayor said, "The time clock will start with the blow of Coach Vargas's whistle. Each contestant will have three minutes to consume as many hot dogs as they can. Any reversal of fortune—and I think we can all figure out what that means—is grounds for disqualification. At the sound of the ending buzzer, contestants must chew and swallow any hot dogs still in the mouth. I will count the remaining dogs and announce the winner. Our esteemed judges are here in case of any dispute. Meriwether Pines, are you ready?"

The crowd went nuts, shouting and screaming.

"Hot dog eaters, are you ready to rumble?"

Becky didn't smile. A simple nod, signaled, Game on! Jimmy nervously nodded his head, yes. They spread bottles of water and other various drinks and condiments in front of the contestants. Becky and Jimmy each had their own plate of hot dogs piled high. Coach Vargas blew the starting whistle, and the big clock began ticking down from three minutes. The crowd grew silent. Jimmy and Becky shoved hot dogs into their mouths. There seemed to be a technique of keeping one ready in the hand while using the other hand to shove the dogs in and cover the mouth.

Lacey thought, *that's probably to prevent a reversal of fortune. Yuck!*

Mr. Man cocked his head to the side and watched the wieners being devoured with intense interest. Anna used her zoom lens to get close-up shots of the frenzied eating. Hot dogs were departing from each contestant's plate and disappearing into their mouths. It was so quiet; you could hear them chewing.

The clock ticked down to 20 seconds.

Becky and Jimmy continued to gorge themselves.

It's a Wienerfeast. It's so gross but I can't look away.

The crowd counted down. "Ten, nine, eight, seven, six—"

Becky was still chewing with her mouth covered and holding an uneaten dog.

The crowd chanted, "Five, four, three—"

An unexpected and brave last-minute strategy, Jimmy uncovered his mouth and shoved one more frankfurter inside.

The crowd screamed, "Two, one!"

BUZZZZZ.

Carrying a portable microphone, the mayor jogged over to the contestant table; He yanked both plates away and counted the remaining hot dogs on each plate. Becky finished chewing. Jimmy was still chomping his last hot dog.

Anna whispered to Lacey, "He's one determined twerp.".

The mayor said, "Becky Danbury, you ate six hot dogs in three minutes."

The crowd cheered.

Becky started to stand up. The mayor walked past Becky and stood behind Jimmy just as he was swallowing his last pulverized bite.

Confused, Becky sat down.

Like Sylvester Stallone in *Rocky*, the mayor grabbed Jimmy's hand and lifted it high above his head. "Jimmy Tang, with a new Meriwether Pines record of consuming seven hot dogs in three minutes, I proclaim that YOU are the new Hot Digitty Dawgalicious Champion!"

The crowd chanted, "Jimmy! Jimmy!".

Jimmy stood up looking shocked and a little green as the mayor led him by the hand to the podium. Standing next to the mayor, Jimmy finally smiled.

Everyone was clapping, including Cousin Anna, who shouted to Lacey. "The twerp did it!".

Mr. Man was jumping up and down, clapping.

Coach Vargas popped up from the judges' table. He rushed over to shake Jimmy's hand and pose for a picture with the hot dog champion and the mayor. Anna and Lacey stood perfectly positioned in front of the podium. Mr. Man held onto Lacey's hat. Lacey had her hands full with Anna's camera bag and equipment.

Anna's camera went click, click.

Mrs. Betty Ford stood up from the judges' table and walked over to congratulate Jimmy and pose for a picture.

Anna's camera went click, click.

In her haste for the photo-opportunity of a lifetime, Mrs. Wigglesworth sprang up from the table, causing her chair to fall backward. She grabbed onto the table and managed to avoid falling. Her crashing chair caught Mr. Man's attention. His little monkey head swiveled in her direction. Mrs. Wigglesworth righted herself, threw her shoulders back, and strode over to stand next to the mayor and Jimmy. She struck the perfect pose for the picture.

Mr. Man homed in on her Victorian Vineyard hat like a thermal-guided missile. This was the hat he had waited for his entire monkey life. This was the holy grail of hats. With the athletic agility that his primate ancestors would have revered, he rocketed off Lacey's hat and landed directly on Mrs. Wigglesworth's charming chapeau.

Anna's camera went click, click, click, click, click, click, click, click.

Mrs. Wigglesworth remained posed.

Coach Vargas, having never taken a picture with a monkey on a lady's hat, leaned in for a picture.

Anna's camera went click, click.

Mrs. Wigglesworth remained posed.

The mayor, having never taken a picture with a monkey on a lady's hat, leaned in for a picture.

Anna's camera went click, click.

Mrs. Wigglesworth remained posed.

Jimmy and Becky, having never taken a picture with a monkey on a lady's hat, leaned in for a picture.

Anna's camera went click, click.

Mrs. Wigglesworth remained posed.

An announcement came over the loudspeakers to "exit immediately to view the U.S. Navy Blue Angels flyover air show."

Mrs. Wigglesworth remained posed.

Everyone on the stage and in the amphitheater filed out to watch the jet demonstration.

Mrs. Wigglesworth remained posed.

Lacey climbed onto the stage and removed Mr. Man from hat heaven, as he was playing with one of the decorative dragonflies.

Mrs. Wigglesworth remained posed.

Lacey slowly waved one hand in front of Mrs. Wigglesworth's face, checking for signs of life.

Mrs. Wigglesworth remained posed.

Lacey thought, *A frozen Wigglesworth is a well-behaved Wigglesworth.*

Lacey and Anna looked at each other and shrugged. They took their stuff and their monkey and left to go watch the air show.

Mrs. Wigglesworth remained posed.

The sound-barrier-breaking thunder of the jets passed over and the crowds cheered.

Mrs. Wigglesworth remained posed.

The crowd spread out onto the commons and watched the fireworks display.

Mrs. Wigglesworth remained posed.

Generations of prestigious Wigglesworth high-society women paraded through her brain waving her mugshot around and pictures of a monkey on her head.

Mrs. Wigglesworth remained posed.

The cleaning crew came and took down the chairs, disassembled the tables, swept around her, and turned the lights out on the stage.

Mrs. Wigglesworth remained posed.

The two-man surveillance team parked in a white van looked

at each other and shook their heads.

"I guess we're stuck here until she leaves."

"Should we call an ambulance?"

44

THE WATCHERS

The following morning, Lacey had all of Mr. Man's things packed and ready to go. Lacey dressed him in a green "I'm more fun than a barrel of monkeys" shirt and said, "I miss you already."

Ding dong.

She carried him to the door. Dr. Bhaiyyani held up the front page of the *Meriwether Tribune* newspaper, dated July 5. On the cover was a huge picture of the mayor standing next to Mrs. Wigglesworth with Mr. Man on her hat. The caption beneath it read "Monkey See Monkey Do." In smaller print it read "Photo courtesy of Anna Chuong."

Lacey thought, *Mrs. Wigglesworth will have bigger problems than monkey troubles after we find out what she's up to!*

Dr. B said, "It looks like Mr. Man was not on his best behavior."

Mr. Man was wiggling like crazy.

Lacey said, "Mr. Man, do you want to see your daddy?" She opened her hand. He let out an excited cry and jumped onto Dr. Bhaiyyani's shoulder.

Dr. Bhaiyyani tried to keep a straight face as Mr. Man planted kisses all over his neck. "I've missed you too, little boy! I see you've been up to some naughty monkey business." Then looking at Lacey, he said, "I apologize for my monkey's bad behavior. I should have warned you about his fondness for hats. From the newspaper photo, that hat looked much too tempting to resist."

"It was definitely different. Dr. B, would you like to come in?"

"Thanks, Lacey, but Mr. Man and I are going to Cape Canaveral, Florida. He has an appointment at the NASA Kennedy Space Center."

"What is he doing there?"

"This little guy is a viable candidate for space travel. He will undergo tests to see if he qualifies for an upcoming space camp next year. I run some of the space camps for NASA Kennedy Space Center using animal astronauts."

"That's amazing! Maxwell, Anna, and I have applications for NASA space camp next spring break and I've filled out an application for my rescue mouse, Mickey. I'll keep my fingers crossed for Mr. Man. Maybe we'll see you guys there! Anytime you need someone to take care of him again, I'm in!"

Lacey looked at Mr. Man's cute monkey face. "Goodbye, Mr. Man."

Mr. Man blew kisses that landed on Lacey's heart and melted it. Lacey said goodbye to Dr. Bhaiyyani and went into the kitchen.

"My little spunky monkey is gone. I'm feeling a little blue." *Speaking of feeling blue, Mickey hasn't been himself lately. He's been moping around and unusually quiet. Maybe he got his little blue mouse feelings hurt when I took Mr. Man to the Fourth-of-July celebration instead of him.*

I've loved Mickey ever since I saw his picture on the Internet and read about those terrible people in that illegal laboratory. It's their fault he's blue and I'm glad that my emails and letters helped to shut that lab down. I'll take him to Maxwell's end of the summer party to cheer him up. But first, it's time for Mickey to go on a mission.

She poured a glass of orange juice and went into Steve's office to grab her walky. A message from Charlotte popped up on the computer screen. Lacey clicked it and a picture of The Tower of London appeared. A message scrolled across the screen. "Her Majesty's Royal Palace and Fortress is a historic castle located on the north bank of the River Thames."

Charlotte's message blinked in red, white, and blue. "These Brits don't celebrate our Independence Day. I didn't want to get locked up in the Tower of London dungeon, so I just lit some sparklers in my uncle's back yard—LAME! I hope your 4th was more eventful and I'll see you soon! Love, Charlotte."

Lacey laughed and said, "Eventful? Yuppers!"

Maxwell's voice came over her walky-talky, "Walky #1 to walky #2, come in."

Lacey answered, "Walky #2, I read you loud and clear. Hi Maxwell, you did so great yesterday! You really rocked the house! Out."

Maxwell said, "Thanks, Lacey. I'm proud of our team. I'm calling because I was reviewing the footage that R3 shot of the show and you wouldn't believe what I saw. Out."

"What? Out?"

"Our two golfers were at the Fourth of July celebration, this time dressed in matching American Flag shirts. Over."

Lacey's heart skipped a beat. "Are you sure it was them?"

Maxwell answered, "Affirmative. Over."

Lacey's heart went from skipping to sprinting. She concentrated on keeping her voice steady. "Were they watching me? Over."

"No. They were definitely watching Mrs. Wigglesworth. They stayed to the end. She was the only person left. Over.

Lacey let out a huge sigh of relief.

Maxwell continued. "I enhanced their images and ran it through my dad's detective image recognition program. They are FBI Agents named Smith and Smith." Over."

"Both of their names are Smith? Over."

"Yeah, weird, I know. Over."

Lacey's brain was spinning faster than a killer tornado. *It's time to take action. The FBI are watching Wigglesworth. BUT SHE'S WATCHING ME.*

She said, "Thanks, Maxwell. That's great news. It's time for the Trias-Lab team to move into action. Call Anna and get her up to speed.? Then I need you both to meet me at Wigglesworth's house at noon. Over."

"We'll be there. Anything else? Over."

"Yes, when I located her house on Google Maps Earth, I discovered a large row of tall bushes across the street from her house. We can hide behind there with our bikes and equipment. Tell Anna to bring the micro-camera she fitted for Mickey and we'll need the monitor to see what he is seeing. Over and out."

The summer's almost over. I need to guarantee that Charlotte returns to a pet sitting business that hasn't been shut down by Wigglesworth.

45

BATTLE PLANS

The team huddled on the grass behind the bushes. Lacey had trouble strapping on Mickey's remote-control harness because he kept trying to wiggle out of it.

He squealed. *"What's going on? I DON'T WANT TO WEAR THIS. Are you going to put me in a BLUE mouse parade? Or make me dance to BLUE Suede Shoes? You'll have to forgive me if I'm not in the mood for any of your mouse-capades."*

Lacey said, "Mickey hold still and stop squealing. It's time to go to work as a rescue mouse."

Mickey's blue fur stood straight up. *"Rescue mouse? Pull the other leg, it plays Jingle Bells. No one will want a BLUE rescue mouse."*

Anna said, "He's acting weird. Why is all his fur standing up? Is this a good time to strap the micro-camera onto his harness? Are you sure he's ready for this?"

Mickey looked at Lacey's face.
Mickey looked at Maxwell's face.
Mickey looked at Anna's face.

"They all look serious. This isn't a joke? I'm still a rescue mouse? A shiny BLUE rescue mouse?"

Lacey said, "He'll be okay. I'll hold him still while you strap it on."

Mickey rolled over on his back with his legs straight in the air. *"Strap it on! Look, I'm completely obedient, timid, mild-mannered—I'm like putty in your hands. Put me in the game! I'm ready to score a touchdown!"*

Maxwell laughed. "Looks like he's ready for the camera, Banana."

Anna attached the tiny camera to the top of his harness and handed him to Lacey. Everyone leaned in and stared at him.

Mickey gave them all the stink eye. *"Stop staring at me. Let's go!"*

Lacey stood up and looked around. No sign of Wigglesworth or anyone else. "I'll run across the street and place him on her front porch. I'll give him the verbal command and enter the corresponding electromagnetic code. I'll run back over here with the remote control and we'll be ready to go."

Lacey ran across the street and placed Mickey on the porch. Lacey and Mickey had practiced this drill a hundred times with a hundred different emergency rescue situations.

This is a RESCUE situation. I'm rescuing Charlotte's Critters!

Lacey entered the code for Liberandum-Surveillance.

Mickey's heart was racing. *"It's undercover agent time!"*

He waited for the pulsing to verify the command. The vibration ended. Mickey squeaked. *"Operation-Surveillance, verified."*

Lacey remained composed and focused. They could do this together. It was time to use their top-secret word. Calmly and clearly, she delivered the command. "Liberandum. Mickey, House Surveillance."

Mickey took off running and screaming, "*Liberandum!*"

Lacey looked around again. *The coast is clear.* She ran across the street and ducked behind the bush.

From behind another bush, two federal agents' eyes were glued to their binoculars.

Agent Smith said, "Was that a mouse?"

Agent Smith said, "Was that a BLUE mouse?"

Lacey sat on the grass between Maxwell and Anna, so they could both see the monitor. Mickey was circling the porch.

Maxwell asked, "What's Mickey doing?"

Lacey said, "He's trained to circle the perimeter for a clear image, then await further commands."

The camera showed American Flags decorating the house everywhere. As he circled around the back, a large inflatable Uncle Sam sat perched by the back door.

Mickey saw the giant Uncle Sam and momentarily veered back. "*You scared the Yankee Doodle out of me! Swimming pools, grills, patio tables, fireworks, but who in the name of Sam puts a giant Yankee Doodle in their backyard?*"

Anna said, "Independence Day overload."

Maxwell said, "Wait a minute! I see something. Can you get him to stop so we can zoom in?"

Lacey entered the stop command. Mickey stopped and Anna showed Lacey how to use the new zoom control.

Lacey said, "Good call, Maxwell!"

A bright orange electric cord ran from the inflatable Uncle Sam directly under the propped open window! Lacey activated the command to 'enter through the window' and they watched Mickey climb up the gutter drain and hop over to the windowsill. And just like that, he was in!

Mickey dropped down to the hardwood floors and landed on

his butt. *"Ouch!"*

He got up and walked to the center of the room. Lacey trained him to do a 360-degree turn when he entered a new room so the camera got a full view.

"He's in her dining room." Said Lacey. "It looks normal to me. Hold it!" She pushed the stop command, and they zoomed in on the wall opposite the window where a large chalkboard was hanging.

Anna read the top line on the chalkboard. "Battle Plans?"

Maxwell let out a low whistle. "We've hit the motherload."

The sound of a car pulling into Mrs. Wigglesworth's driveway shattered the silent street. Maxwell moved some branches around to get a better look. "She's home!"

Lacey said, "I've got to get Mickey out of there. But first, I'll zoom in and snap pictures of the board and the surrounding area."

She pushed a few buttons then sent the electronic command, Abort Mission.

Mickey heard the front door slam at the same time he received the command. He scampered to the window and climbed the curtain to the windowsill. He heard footsteps approaching and slid under the windowsill. *"That was a close call."*

Mickey raced around the house and back to the front into Lacey's hands. "Mickey! You did it!"

Lacey met Maxwell and Anna behind the bush and all three took off on their bikes. Nobody said a word as they zoomed past a group of bushes concealing two bewildered FBI Agents.

"Can we charge them with breaking and entering?"

"We could arrest the mouse."

"The Washington office would re-locate us to the North Pole."

"Good point."

"Let's find out what Wilma Wigglesworth is up to."

46

SLIPPERY SITUATION

While Maxwell and Anna reviewed the surveillance video, Lacey was at her final Charlotte's Critters visit.

Lacey parked her bicycle in a bike rack at the Luxury Life Apartment Homes. She put on her Crittercam hat and thought about grabbing her windbreaker. The sky looked ominous. She decided she had enough stuff to carry and left it with her bike. Lacey opened the file, pulled out the key, and put it around her neck.

Turning to the file page, she noted that the dog named Jack had boxes "DOG", "WALK", "WATER", and "TREATS" marked. Lacey scanned down to the chicken scratch file note.

Jack ra_i_g-stop_heavy

In an attempt to gain any level of comprehension, she read the note out loud three times to herself, each time trying a different pronunciation or possible combination of letters.

"Jackerag? stop heavy."

"Jack—ragsssstop heavy."

"Jack is—topheavy? Ugh!"

Ladies and gentlemen, our contestant Lacey Honeycut is here to play Spin the Mystery Note, give her a round of applause.

This crucial note might as well have been written in Swahili. Lacey used her Jedi mind powers to transmit a message of gratitude to Charlotte's Uncle Conway for his penmanship tutelage. She clipped her walky on her belt and strapped on her backpack. Jack's apartment was on the first floor. The brand-new apartment complex was in the center of town and decorated with lush landscaping and fountains.

Lacey unlocked the door. A large black-and-white cow greeted her.

What kind of dog is this? He's got cowhide markings but obviously he's not part cow.

Lacey was usually good at identifying breeds.

I'm stumped.

The gigantic dog of confusing lineage stretched out his front and rear legs and gave a long, loud yawn followed by what sounded like—and she wouldn't swear to this, Rooby Roo.

Lacey said, "Walky-time Jack! Ready for your walk?" He gave a small wag of his long tail and sauntered over to Lacey. Jack's nose went nuts, inspecting Lacey's feet while she was petting his back.

"All right Inspector Gadget, let's get moving before it rains."

Lacey retrieved Jack's leash from the door hook and attached it to his collar. He showed every sign of being an obedient and calm dog. Thank goodness, because he weighed more than Lacey. "Let's go, big boy." Once outside, Lacey and Jack headed toward the central hub of town a few blocks up. Luxury Life sat in the heart of shopping, fast-food restaurants, and other conveniences. Jack the cow wasn't exactly a sprinter—more of a stand-in-one-spot-smeller. He seemed to enjoy their stroll and had accomplished "his job". As they turned to head back, the sky was darkening.

Little droplets of rain hit Lacey's face. Rather than go back the way they came, she took a shortcut across the big intersection on the main road. They could beat the rain by taking the crosswalk. It was close to dinnertime and rush hour traffic was at its peak. Lacey pushed the crosswalk button. Jack stood there with her, waiting for the walking person to light up. Just as the sign blinked "*WALK, WALK*", the wind and rain picked up.

As Lacey and Jack started to cross the street, the sky opened up. Hard pellets of water struck Lacey and Jack, smacking on the surrounding pavement.

I don't mind getting wet as long as it's not lightning. Jack's apartment is close by. I can towel him off when we get back.

Jack had other ideas.

As the rain intensified, Jack planted his butt on the pavement in the middle of the crosswalk surrounded by bumper-to-bumper traffic.

"Jack!" Lacey pulled Jack's leash upward to get him to stand up. He looked away from her.

"Jack, giddy-up cowboy!"

Nothing. Jack didn't budge.

They were both already soaking wet.

Lacey walked around to face his head. She spread her feet wide for leverage. She wrapped her arms around the trunk of his chest area and shouted, "Heave ho Jack!"

As she struggled to pull him forward, Jack changed from sitting to lying down. All four legs split off in different directions, causing Lacey to fall backward on her butt.

SPLAT!

She landed in a huge puddle. "Ouch! Jack! You're too heavy!"

At that precise moment, Charlotte's note became crystal clear to her.

Jack raining stop heavy.

"SERIOUSLY CHARLOTTE!!!!"

Lacey stood up and heard the blinking crosswalk sign buzzing. Through the rain, the walking man flashed red. "Do Not Walk". Lacey was hoping Jack couldn't read signs. She leaned down low and made eye contact with Jack.

Eye contact is vital for dog whispering.

In her most calm yet commanding I-am-your-Alpha voice, she said, "Jack stand up!"

Jack broke eye contact and stubbornly looked away from her.

Drivers were getting impatient. They had the green signal but couldn't move because of a soggy girl and her cow-like dog. Deciding on a different technique, Lacey walked around to his rear end. She squatted down with her face lined up to his tail and backside. She took a deep breath and shoved with all her might.

Nothing. Jack didn't budge.

Lacey walked back in front of him and tried dragging him while whistling and calling in her most fake, high-pitched cheerful voice. "Here Jack, here Jack."

No success.

As the deluge continued, car horns were tooting. At first, it was one or two polite beep-beeps. Then it grew louder with more horns blaring.

BEEEEEP! BEEEEEP! BEEEEEP!

A man shouted, "Get out of the road!"

Holding Jack's leash in her left hand, she pulled her walky from her belt clip. Visibility was nonexistent as rain poured from the top of her Crittercam hat, caked her eyelashes, and dripped past the end of her nose. She hoped the camera was waterproof. The last thing she needed was for it to emit sparks, causing her head to erupt into fire. Her hands were slippery and started to shake.

Lacey pushed the 3 to call Maxwell. At least she thought she pushed the 3. She shouted into the walky, "Help! Jack is down. I repeat, Jack is down and I can't move him. We're in the middle of the intersection of Fifth and Main—require immediate assistance—over!" Lacey held the walky in her left hand, hoping for a response. The red light blinked once then went off.

The battery just died. Seriously? I must have forgotten to put it on the charger last night. Lacey looked down at Jack and tried one more time to rally the obstinate dog.

"Jack, I've got treats for you at home and a warm towel. Who's a good boy!"

Jack ignored her.

She looked around and could see even more cars backing up in the street. The sky was so dark, the cars' headlights were on. A fresh barrage of stuck driver's complaints assaulted her ears over the pounding of the rain. Lacey got an earful of insults.

"Hey genius, you're blocking traffic!"

"You're making me late for my appointment!"

"Get out of the street, you birdbrain!"

With the back of her hand that was still desperately clinging to the useless walky-talky, Lacey wiped nervous perspiration and raindrops from her face. Where were Maxwell and Anna? Had they heard her call for help? The sound of approaching sirens jarred Lacey. As they grew closer, they drowned out the pounding rain, car engines, and relentless horns. She wondered if someone had an accident in the middle of this traffic jam. Then like a lightning bolt—it struck her.

I didn't call Maxwell and Anna on the walky. In my panic, I must have pushed 33 instead of 3.

Lacey Honeycut had mistakenly called for immediate help from all nearby emergency vehicles. She looked down at Jack. "This is your fault, Jack. You're a stubborn ox!"

Jack raised his head and looked at her, unimpressed. He looked her up and down then turned his head away again.

The storm was moving past and dissolved into a drizzle. An ambulance screeched to a stop, lights, and sirens blazing. It parked on the sidewalk close to the crosswalk. Lacey waved her walky-talky frantically in the air. Two attendants got out and pulled a stretcher from the back. They ran toward Lacey and Jack and into the intersection.

One of the men asked Lacey, "Where are you hurt?"

Embarrassed, Lacey said, "It's not me. I'm fine. It's him!" She raised Jack's leash in the air. All eyes followed down the leash to the prostrate cow-dog.

The attendant asked, "Was he hit by a car?"

"No." (She almost said, I wish.)

"What's wrong with him?" asked the bewildered man.

"He's stubborn! He's obstinate! He hates the rain! He's sulking, and he's as big as a cow!"

The other guy said, "So he's just parked?"

Lacey said, "Yes, illegally parked. I can't get him to move out of the road."

"Is he friendly?"

"I don't know about friendly, but he won't bite you."

The two attendants looked at each other.

They looked at the dog.

They looked at the terrible traffic jam.

They looked at the stretcher, then locked eyes.

One of them shrugged his shoulders and said, "Why not?"

They placed the stretcher next to Jack. Standing on each side of him, they lifted the heavy dog up onto the stretcher. Jack seemed to find the stretcher comfortable and rolled over on his back with his legs straight up in the air. Lacey followed the stretcher out of the middle of the road and back onto the safety of the sidewalk just as the rain let up.

Maxwell's dad pulled up and Maxwell jumped out of the car. "My dad heard about this on his radio. I've been trying to reach you. Are you okay?"

Lacey grabbed Jack's leash. HE STOOD UP. She rolled her eyes and said to Maxwell, "Now that it's not raining, we're fine. Why were you trying to reach me?"

"We reviewed the videos, and it's not good."

"Walk with me back to Jack's and tell me what you found."

Maxwell waved to his dad. As he walked a soggy girl and a soggy dog to the apartment, he told Lacey about Mrs. Wigglesworth's BATTLE PLAN. "Lacey, I told my dad everything, and he pulled some reports. She's trying to get Charlotte's business license taken away. She also plans on leaving town so she doesn't have to testify against the guy who blew up the house. But here's the worst part—"

"—There's a worst part?"

"She's planning on crashing my party and causing some kind of trouble."

Lacey said, "We have to report this to Agent Smith and Agent Smith."

47

PARTY PLANS

Lacey, Mickey, Mom, and Steve were the first to arrive at Maxwell's house for the party. Petey stayed home with a babysitter because it was past his bedtime. On the car ride over, Lacey finally spilled the beans to Mom and Steve. She spilled ALL the beans; Wigglesworth, pets gone wild, Mickey's surveillance mission, and sharing their information with FBI Agents, Smith & Smith.

They sat in the car in front of Maxwell's house.

Mom said, "I wish you would have told us about this sooner. Do we need to worry about the party today?"

"We'll be fine. If she shows up, a plan is in place." Lacey looked out the window at Maxwell's front yard. A red carpet was rolled out in the yard, leading to the front door. "Look! They rolled out the red carpet for the party! Let's go!"

The door was partially open with a note, "Welcome friends! Come in and follow the red carpet for our End of the Summer Pizza and Ice Cream Blast." Lacey placed Mickey on her shoulder for a good view of the festivities. The red carpet wound through the living room and straight out to a large backyard.

Lacey gasped when she saw the magical transformation. The usual backyard stuff was gone. They had moved the soccer goals, a croquet set, lawnmower, even the trampoline. The red carpet cut a path on the grass straight out to a giant movie screen hanging between two large pine trees. White folding chairs lined each side of the red carpet, lit by flaming bamboo tiki torches.

Maxwell's parents, Marty and Amber, approached. Marty said, "Steve and Sara, we're so glad you could make it. Our kids have had QUITE a summer together."

Mom raised her eyebrows. "You can say that again.".

Marty looked at Mickey. "Is that the blue mouse I keep hearing about?"

"Yes, he has Argyrosis, a condition that turned his fur blue. Silver chemical exposure caused it in a lab. I LOVE his extraordinary blue color."

Marty said, "I agree.".

Mickey nudged Lacey's neck. *"She thinks I'm extraordinary."*

Lacey said, "Mr. and Mrs. Ayce, this backyard is a radical change! This must have taken forever!"

Mrs. Ayce replied, "I'm glad you like it."

Lacey said, "Like it? No way! I love it! Hey, where's Maxwell?"

Mr. Ayce said, "Maxwell and Harry are busy tweaking some final configurations with the audiovisual equipment for the movie. You know what a perfectionist he is with that stuff. You can just hang out here while the guests arrive."

Mrs. Ayce said, "We're all going to watch a movie together when the sun goes down. We've got three food stations set up. That's my favorite station." She pointed at a red cart on wheels with a green-striped umbrella over it. A black-and-white sign hung from the umbrella. "Fresh cranked ice cream. Help yourself."

Lacey asked, "Homemade ice cream?"

"That's right. Maxwell and I made it last night with the ice cream crank he invented last summer. It works better than any fancy expensive ice cream maker at a fraction of the cost, and you know how Maxwell's dad loves to save money."

"Lacey!" Anna ran toward her with her parents and brothers following like wayward ducklings. She hugged Lacey tight and whispered in her ear, "Is the plan in place?"

Lacey whispered back, "All parties are ready and waiting.".

Lacey greeted Anna's parents, Mr. and Mrs. Chuong. Anna's brothers spied the ice cream cart and veered off screeching "ice cream!"

"Where's Maxwell?" Anna asked Lacey.

"His dad said he and Harry are working on some kind of technical issues for the movie."

"Do you know what movie we are watching tonight?"

Lacey replied, "No, but I hope it's funny. You know how much I love comedies."

Anna pulled Lacey further away from the parents and whispered, "Can we really pull this off?"

48

PARTY SURPRISE

The sun was setting and Lanterns magically lit up the garden. People were moving around, piling food on their plates, and talking in small groups. Lacey, Anna, Valencia, and Vanessa were at the pizza station. Mickey was on his second round of pizza crust.

He wiped the crumbs from his mouth. "*I had no idea how hungry being a secret agent BLUE rescue mouse could make me. This pizza crust tastes just like the pizza my Papa made back in the Bronx.*"

A voice from behind them said, "You girls got that much room in your bellies?" Charlotte came up behind them and put her arms around Lacey and Anna. "I missed you so much this summer! I can't wait to show you all my pictures from my trip."

She gave Lacey a big hug. "I can't thank you enough for saving Charlotte's Critters. Without you to cover, I would have lost my business. I spoke to my clients, and they said that it seemed like everything went smoothly. That's so great that you didn't have any problems!"

Lacey and Anna both stifled a laugh.

Charlotte spotted Mickey. "I love your blue mouse! He's soooo cool, he could be a TV star!"

Mickey felt pride swell up in his little mouse chest. "*TV star—Mickey Antonio Mouse, ACTOR. It's got a certain ring to it. My buddies in New York might not accept Blue Antonio, but Lacey and her friends think I'm the cat's meow. Maybe blue is the new black. I'M the mouse to watch. Move over MICKEY. Blue might be Minnie's favorite color. I guess I'll stick around in Meriwether Pines for a while.*"

A bell started ringing. Maxwell appeared standing in front of the movie screen. He was wearing a tuxedo with tails, a white shirt, and red bow tie. He spoke into a wireless microphone and addressed the crowd. "Friends and neighbors, fellow students and teachers, coaches and parents, welcome! Please take your food and drinks and find a seat. This is a party to celebrate our summer vacation. I have put together a surprise for you on the movie screen. Thank you for being here. Sit back and enjoy the movie."

Parked outside in front of Maxwell's house, Agent Smith and Agent Smith sat in their car watching the monitor loaned to them by the Trias lab kids.

"These kids are pretty smart. It was a brilliant suggestion. to program the R3 drone to watch from above. If she's here, we'll see her."

"I still don't understand how we lost her in the first place."

"Let's not go over this again."

"I'm just saying, we saw her go into the house with the mouse then you told me to watch the house because you had to step into the woods to 'water the plants.'"

"I'm sorry! It was a long stakeout. But you were responsible for watching her."

"I only took my eyes off the house for a few minutes. What can I say? Nature was calling my name too."

"As long as we catch her today, we don't have to let the Washington office know about that small snafu."

"We're lucky the kids called us and sent us the Battle Plan evidence and the photo of her packed suitcase sitting right there."

"I'll kick myself if she gets away. We need her to testify against the counterfeiting ring or the whole case falls apart."

Back at the party, it had grown dark. The lantern lights lit the path to their seats. Lacey, Anna, and Charlotte walked to the front row where chairs with paper signs read "Reserved for Lacey, Anna, Charlotte, and Maxwell". Lacey settled Mickey on her shoulder. Charlotte handed Lacey a hot-pink envelope. On the front, "Lacey" was written in beautiful calligraphy.

Charlotte said, "Lacey, my parents, and I want to give this to you to thank you for taking care of my business while I was away."

Lacey took the envelope. She took a quick peek inside and caught her breath when she saw the amount on the check made out to Lacey Honeycut. "Thanks, Charlotte. It really wasn't any trouble at all." As the lights went out and the movie screen lit up, nobody could see the wide grin that spread slowly across Lacey's face all the way up to her sparkling blue eyes.

One step closer to owning Lancelot.

Maxwell came over and sat in his reserved seat.

He looks so handsome and grown-up in his tuxedo.

He held a remote control in one hand and the wireless mike in the other. He looked at the girls and winked. "Ready?"

PARTY SURPRISE

Maxwell pushed the button on the remote. The movie screen lit up. A picture that Lacey recognized from the first pool party of the summer was on the screen. Lacey, Anna, and Maxwell sat at the umbrella table with their arms around each other and Mickey on Lacey's shoulder.

It's our first summer picture together from the pool party!
A title scrolled up.

<u>*Lacey Honeycut's Hilarious, Disastrous, Furry, Summer Vacation*</u>
Starring Lacey Honeycut
Guest Starring Maxwell Ayce and Anna (Banana) Chuong

Lacey and Anna looked at Maxwell. He leaned back and crossed his arms with a smug grin on his face. They all looked back at the screen. He made the movie from live feeds on the Crittercam. Maxwell spliced the scenes in order chronologically and edited the movie with photos and funny sayings.

Four blocks away, Wilma Wigglesworth waited impatiently at a traffic light.

49

PARTY POOPER

Agent Smith and Agent Smith sat in their black unmarked sedan watching the drone monitor scan the party and the house with night vision cameras. A warning blinked three times, "Recharge battery". The monitor went dark.

"We've lost our feed."

"Let's go inside and find a wall socket to recharge it."

They exited the car in matching black suits, with white shirts and black skinny ties. They kept their Wayfarer sunglasses on, even though it was dark out. Their freshly shined shoes clicked up the sidewalk to Maxwell's house. They entered the open front door and followed the sounds out to the backyard. A movie was just starting to play, and everyone was seated with their backs to them. Tall Smith spotted an electrical outlet by a table of food. "What do you say we use this downtime for some chow while we're waiting for it to recharge?"

Short and Stout Smith picked up a cupcake. "A simple reassignment of unreported acquisitions."

They stuffed their mouths with food and watched the movie Short Smith burst out laughing. "These kids made this movie themselves? They are talented squirts!"

Tall and Skinny Smith popped cubes of cheese into his mouth and replied, "I wish my nephew spent more time doing stuff like this rather than collecting stamps."

Shorty Smith squirted a can of Cool Whip directly into his mouth and mumbled back, "uhhumm um."

Out front, Mrs. Wigglesworth pulled her car up to the address listed in her very thick notebook, titled "Grievances and Atrocities Besmirching the Good Name and Reputation of Mrs. Wilma Wren Wigglesworth-BATTLE PLAN."

According to her online research, this was Maxwell Ayce's place of residence, and this is where they would all be for their stupid party. When she was done with them, they wouldn't have anything to celebrate about. She wore black from head to toe, just like a cat-burglar. She didn't plan on breaking in, but then again, she didn't really have a specific plan for the party, yet.

On July fifth, when she stepped onto her porch to retrieve the *Meriwether Tribune* and faced a picture of herself on the cover with a monkey on her head, she had blown her gasket. Correction, first she fainted, then when she regained consciousness, she blew her gasket. It was at that moment that she affirmed in a Powervoice (albeit a shaky and sobbing Powervoice), "Create a Battle Plan! Take no prisoners! Show no mercy!" Now she waited in her car and watched more guests arrive. "Think, Wilma, think!"

She got out and tippy-toed ran along the side of Maxwell's yard. She considered breaking down the front door but decided a sneakier approach would be better. She looked at the backyard wood fence and tried to gauge how tall it was. Could she climb over that? She was about to try when she realized the gate door was open.

She tippy-toe ran along the edge of the fence and ducked behind the movie screen. Everyone was laughing and clapping at the stupid movie—which apparently starred Lacey Honeycut and her two friends. She muttered, "They're frauds and hooligans and they're dangerous to society.

If it wasn't for Lacey, I never would have discovered that fake money house, nearly got killed by an explosion, ended up with a mug shot and a monkey on my head. She has made a complete spectacle of me and now I am forced to leave town or testify in court against criminals. What can I do to pay her back?"

She crouched behind the screen. "Think, Wilma, think!"

As the movie played, there wasn't a quiet moment in the crowd of family and friends. Everyone laughed and howled at the summer's exploits. People were literally falling off their lawn chairs from cracking up.

Agents Smiths were holding their sides with gut-splitting hysterics.

The final scene was the craziest, with Lacey standing in the middle of the street surrounded by ambulances, fire trucks, and police cars. In one hand, the soaking wet girl held her walky-talky, waving it back and forth. In the other hand, she held the leash of stubborn Jack.

The song "Who Let the Dogs Out" began to play. As the movie ended, still shots of Jack being taken to the sidewalk on a stretcher led to even more uproarious laughter by the crowd. Credits rolled.

"Special thanks to Charlotte of Charlotte's Critters and her wonderful clients."

"Special Guest Appearances, Mickey the blue mouse, Gracie and Buddy, Munchkin the cat, Dr. Evil and Shadow, Brutus,

Stella, and Booger, Jack, Mr. Man, Dr. B, the Wild Roos, Jimmy, Valencia and Vanessa, Mrs. Betty Ford, the mayor of Meriwether Pines and a dancing hot dog."

"Disclaimer: No animals or people were injured, abused, neglected, sprayed with deer repellent, or forced to dance the Dougy."

The movie ended and the lights went on. Maxwell pushed his remote and the movie screen rolled back up revealing MRS. WILMA WREN WIGGLESWORTH squatting down on the ground. She looked around like a deer caught in the headlights. The crowd started laughing and pointing at her, thinking it was still part of the show.

Lacey yelled, "It's Wigglesworth! Don't let her get away!"

Mrs. Wigglesworth took off running back toward the open fence door.

Lacey held onto Mickey and ran through the crowd. She bumped right into two startled FBI agents and shouted, "Where's the monitor?"

Agent Smith pointed to the charging screen. Lacey grabbed the monitor and swiped the screen. She touched, "Settings", "Dronebot", "Offensive", "Netting", then swiped back to the camera zoom just as Anna and Maxwell arrived next to her.

In the viewfinder, they could see Wilma running toward her car.

Lacey said, "Maxwell if I get the drone close enough can I activate 'Net-Capture'?

Maxwell said, "It should work. I'll go down to the lab and make sure the main-frame is communicating, and the net is properly loaded." Maxwell ran into the house.

Anna pointed at the monitor. "She's not getting in her car. It looks like she locked herself out."

Mrs. Wigglesworth circled her car one more time. She looked right and left for an escape route.

Lacey said, "I'm moving the drone closer to her. Let's go out front so I can get a visual of the drone and the target. Anna, hold Mickey and follow me."

Lacey ran into the house followed by Anna, Agents Smiths and EVERYONE ELSE.

Mrs. Wigglesworth was in a complete panic. She stood by her car mumbling to herself. "Stupid car, stupid keys. I must have dropped them in the yard. Stupid, Stupid, Stupid." She heard a strange helicopter sound above her head and looked up. A drone was losing altitude above her. "What is going on?"

Lacey Honeycut burst out the front door screaming, "You're not getting away!"

Wilma screamed, "Oh, yes I am!" She took two steps to the right and then decided to turn left.

The whirling blades grew louder.

Lacey moved R3 lower and activated the Arrest Warning command.

A creepy robot voice said, "This is R3. You are under arrest. Put your hands behind your head and kneel down."

"What?" Wilma looked up into a bright spotlight and squinted her eyes.

"R3, do your stuff!" Lacey activated the net.

Whoosh!

A door opened on the bottom of the flying robot and released a large sticky net. Mrs. Wigglesworth fell to the sidewalk caught in the netting. Like a fly stuck on flypaper, every time she moved, it stuck to her more. She looked up at Lacey, then Anna and Mickey. She screamed, "BLUE RAT!"

Maxwell appeared next, looking down at her, then the FBI

agents.

Agent Smith said, "Do you have your lucky handcuffs?"

Agent Smith pulled the cuffs from his belt. "Right here, Shock and Awe."

Agent Smith helped Mrs. Wigglesworth get free from the net. "It's time for Shock and Awe."

Agent Smith pulled out a shiny badge. "Mrs. Wilma Wren Wigglesworth, we meet again. I am Agent Smith, an officer of the Federal Bureau of Investigation. I am placing you under arrest for evading FBI agents and refusing to testify in a federal counterfeiting case. Please place your hands together in front of you."

Mrs. Wigglesworth lowered her head and put her sticky hands together.

Mickey jumped from Anna to Lacey's shoulder and yelled, *"That's what you get for being mean to MY Lacey! I place the Curse of the Bambino on you!*

TO BE CONTINUED...

Read Chapter One of the next Lacey Honeycut Adventure:

LACEY HONEYCUT'S HOLLYWOOD, ALIEN, ANIMAL-WRANGLING CHRISTMAS VACATION

Lacey Honeycut sat perched at the desk, assessing the fluffy snowflakes that had begun to fall outside her window.

A perfect day for the beach—where I'm going.

For what seemed like the bazillionth time, she scowled at the telephone, urging it to ring.

PARTY POOPER

The phone just sat there, as lazy as her white Persian cat Drowsy,

snoozing on her lap.

Useless phone.

Her blue mouse Mickey sprinted on his exercise wheel in front of her, on the brink of breaking all rodent Olympic speed records.

Geez, he's going to give himself a heart attack.

Lacey's eyes followed the phone cord to the wall socket.

Okay phone, you're plugged in. You have my permission to ring.

The suspense was killing her! Lacey's brain was spinning as fast as Mickey's squeaky wheel. Her fingers fidgeted with her computer keyboard, typing the words "Ring, Ring, Ring, Big Surprise????"—and then backspaced and erased them.

I can't believe this day is finally here! Adios snowy Meriwether Pines. Hello warm and sunny Hollywood, California! The perfect winter vacation to visit my real dad AND I'm turning twelve on Christmas Eve! And Dad says there's an even bigger surprise. Newsflash! My flight is in a few hours. It's WAY past time for the big movie-magic reveal!

Lacey's dad was a famous movie director and a master of surprises. Like a yipping Jack Russell Terrier, Lacey had been jumping and snapping for a treat, always slightly out of reach from her dad's teasing, I've-got-a-surprise-for-you hand. Since last July, no matter how many times she jumped and yipped, her begging fell on sealed lips. Not even one clue from her dad.

Geez! Enough already! Give it up!

Ding dong!

Ah-hah! That explains the silent phone! My surprise is ringing the doorbell!

Drowsy lifted her head and decided it was too much effort to run to the door. She was a cat, not a watchdog. She pushed her head further into Lacey's stomach and purred.

Ding dong!

A family of butterflies fluttered all around in Lacey's stomach. She froze in anticipation.

Mom will get the door. I'll sit here and act cool.

Ding dong!

Frightened by the loud bell, Mickey missed a step on his exercise wheel. "*Cheese and Cra—OUCH!*" He tripped over his tail and tumbled onto the hard desktop. Lying flat on his back, he groaned, "*Cheese and Crackers! Will SOMEONE answer the door or does the MOUSE have to do everything in this house? I hope you're happy now! I've lost my runner's Zen. I mean I was really in the zone, training like a prize-fighter.*" He stood up and wiped sweat from his forehead. "*I'm sweating bullets. Anybody got a towel for the workout king?*"

Lacey nervously drummed her fingers on the desk.

Mickey stood next to her tapping fingers and gave her his best stink-eye. "*Why do I bother? The only one who understands what I'm saying is the cat. All Lacey hears is squeak squeak. My New York, Boston mouse family's Curse of the Bambino continues. That curse haunted the Boston Red Sox for 86 years when they traded away the Bambino, Babe Ruth. Has anyone ever heard of a mouse that is only understood by CATS? Anyone?*"

He hopped down onto Lacey's lap and landed on Drowsy who paid absolutely no attention to him. Using the cat's furry tail to mop up his perspiration, Mickey said, "*Drowsy, my feline friend, I always knew you would come in handy for something.*"

Drowsy lifted her head briefly and half-smiled at Mickey as if to say, "That's what friends are for."

PARTY POOPER

Ding dong!

From upstairs, Lacey heard the front door open and then close. The butterflies fluttered in her stomach.

Settle down belly.

Footsteps marched up the stairs and the door to her bedroom opened. Lacey's mom held out a small package wrapped with express mail tape. "It's from your father," she said.

Like a two-year-old reclaiming a toy and screaming, "*Mine! Mine!*" Lacey jumped up to snatch the package, causing Drowsy and Mickey to plop to the floor.

Drowsy's big blue eyes opened wide, followed by a sharp "*Meow-ouch!*" She lifted the chin of her adorable smooshed-up face, looking highly offended.

Mickey stood up and shook his scrunched-up fist at Lacey. "*You gotta show more respect to the mouse! That was just rude!*"

Lacey glanced at the pile of cat and mouse and muttered, "Oops, sorry."

She squeezed the package in her hands. "It's daddy's big surprise!"

The express mail tape was stubbornly serious about its job. Lacey couldn't pry it loose, even using her teeth.

Lacey's mother held out a pair of scissors, "Lacey, manners."

"Sorry," Lacey mumbled, "Thanks."

As Lacey cut away the wrapping, Mom asked, "Are you all packed and ready for your flight this afternoon?"

"Yes I am. Yes! Yes! Yes!"

Mom scrunched up her nose and covered her ears. "Lacey don't shout. I heard you the first time."

Lacey waved a brand-new cell phone in front of her mom and hopped up and down like a bunny on a sugar-high. "The other yeses were for this. Daddy got me a cell phone!"

The new cell phone began to ring, playing "Little Saint Nick" by the Beach Boys. Lacey and her dad absolutely loved that song. Lacey answered the phone and screamed into it, "Daddy—No way! A cell phone! Thank you! Thank you!"

Dad said, "Elfie (that was his nickname for her because she was born on Christmas Eve), I'm so glad your phone got there in time. By the way, there's still a *bigger* surprise."

Lacey screeched, "Bigger?"

"Yes, we'll get to that in a minute. We weren't getting you a phone until you turned thirteen, but your mom and I discussed it, and we thought it would be much safer for you to travel with your own cell phone. That way we can both reach you whenever we need to. We have agreed that you are responsible enough to take care of it and not lose it. Right?"

The sparkling Scooby Doo cell phone cover held Lacey in a Rooby-Roo love trance. She caressed Scooby's face and stared into his big brown eyes.

"Responsible, right?" repeated Dad.

Lacey planted a kiss right on Scooby's sparkly nose. "Absolutely!"

"Okay, because we're going to be *very* busy while you're here, and we won't always be together. Are you listening to me?"

Lacey snapped out of her dazzling doggy trance and quickly praised her parents like well-behaved pups. "Great thinking, Mom and Dad."

She flashed a huge Lacey grin and gave a thumbs-up to her mom. Then, to demonstrate her total commitment to proper cell phone care, she waved her fingers across her heart. "I cross my heart and hope to die, stick a needle in my eye."

"Lacey-Lu!" said Mom. "You know I don't like that saying."

Realizing she may have pushed the parent training thing a

little too far, she said, "Sorry, Mom". Then she asked, "Hey Dad, what do you mean, we won't always be together?"

Dad's deep voice boomed from the speaker. "That's part two of your surprise. Elfie, I have a showbiz Christmas present for you. Remember I told you last summer that I am directing a teen science fiction movie? It's called *My Pet Is an Alien Imposter.*

Lacey's heart pittered and pattered. "*Alien Imposter*, yes."

"We are using lots of animal actors in the movie."

Mickey's little mouse ears perked up and he started grooming himself when he heard animal actors.

Drowsy had recovered from her floor dump and was sleeping again, dreaming of a world where a blue mouse didn't order her around.

Dad delivered the surprise. "Elfie, Congratulations! You have been hired as the second assistant junior animal wrangler on the movie!"

Lacey was silent for approximately—zero seconds, before she shouted out, *"No way!"*

"Way!" Dad said. "We will be shooting lots of scenes at different locations including Disneyland California."

"No way!"

"Way! —and you'll be working under the direction of one of the best animal trainers in the business—and, a personal friend of mine, Texan, Big Ed."

"No Way!"

Mom was still standing next to her when the useless phone started ringing on the desk. Ring, ring—I'm useful again. She answered it and held it out for Lacey. "It's for you. It's Anna. She says it's an emergency."

"Hold on, Dad." Lacey grabbed the receiver. "Anna, are you

okay?"

"Lacey, sorry to use the e-word with your mom but you're my best friend in the whole wide world so I just have to tell you my news right away! I'm going to California for winter vacation to visit my cousin Bea. Can you believe it? We're going to take the Hollywood Tour of the Stars, shop till we drop, go to Disneyland, and—"

Lacey cut in. "You're going to Disneyland? So am I!"

"No way!" said Anna.

"Way!" said Lacey.

"Hello? Lacey, are you still there?" asked Dad.

Lacey said into her cell phone, "Yes, dad, sorry. Hold on."

The computer alerted a Skype call coming in. "Call for Lacey Honeycut from Maxwell."

"Hang on Anna," said Lacey.

Maxwell's image came up on the screen. He wore a white science coat and sat in the Trias-Lab, a basement laboratory he shared with Lacey and Anna.

"Maxwell, what's up?"

Maxwell said, "R3, show Lacey the offer letter."

A creepy looking spider drone hovered and held a document up to the camera. Maxwell's weird dronebot always flew around the lab, obeying all his instructions.

Lacey leaned closer to the screen. "Sorry, I can't read that and I'm on two other calls.

Maxwell commanded, "R3, report back to base." The drone flew off with the paper. "Ever since I got my FAA drone operator's license, I've been applying for drone internship jobs. Hold onto your hat because I've officially landed my first drone aerial cinematography job! I'm the second assistant, drone cinematographer for a movie filming in California over our vacation. It's called *My Pet—*.

Lacey interrupted. "*Is an Alien Imposter?*"

Maxwell's blue eyes narrowed to a squint. He leaned so close to the Skype camera that Lacey could count the freckles on his face. Raising one eyebrow, he asked, "How did you know that?"

"That's the movie my dad is directing. I'm working on it too—as junior animal wrangler!"

"No way!" said Maxwell.

"Way!" said Lacey.

"Hello? Lacey?" It was Anna. "Are you still there?"

Dad piped in. "Elfie, can you hear me?"

Lacey held one phone to each ear. "Dad, Maxwell, and Anna! We're all going to be in California at the same time!"

"No way!" said Dad.

"No way!" said Anna.

"No way!" said Maxwell.

"Way!" shouted Lacey.

Mickey scanned the room for his travel cage. "*Hollywood, here I come!*"

In an office far away from Meriwether Pines, a computer identified a flight booked for Lacey Honeycut and began chirping away printing out a twenty-page report. A tall man with a bushy mustache scanned the documents and handed them to a short man with a bushy mustache.

In an, I'm-concerned-that-the-world-might-end, tone of voice, the tall mustached man said, "Looks like we've got suspicious activity in the small town of Meriwether Pines—again."

The short mustached man nodded.

"I thought that case was locked up tight," said the tall man.

"Apparently, not tight enough. The Wigglesworth woman was placed in a witness protection program far away so she couldn't cause trouble for those three kids again. She was sent to—.

"California!" said, tall man as he packed his surveillance equipment into his black duffel bag. He grabbed the files marked "Top Secret" and his GPS device. "Have the car pulled around. We've got to get to the airport, presto!"

END OF CHAPTER ONE

A NOTE FROM LACEY HONEYCUT.
Hello YAY-CATIONERS!!!
I hope you LOVED this Lacey Honeycut Adventure!!!
Please post FIVE STAR REVIEWS for my books—EVERYWHERE to keep the YAY-CATION going!!! Lacey

Lisa M. Stackpole
Author

About the Author

Lisa M. Stackpole has worked as a model, actor, animal trainer, and commercial scriptwriter. Her love of laughter, animals, travel, and adventure are reflected in her writings. Lisa resides in Atlanta, Georgia with her furry children.

You can connect with me on:
- https://instagram.com/LACEYHONEYCUT
- http://www.laceyhoneycut.com

Subscribe to my newsletter:
- http://lisastackpole.com

Also by Lisa M. Stackpole

Lacey Honeycut's Hollywood Alien Animal-Wrangling Christmas Vacation

Lacey Honeycut's Fantastic Galactic Space Camp Spring Break

More Lacey Honeycut adventures to come.

Please comment on our Instagram and YouTube pages if you have a vacation idea for Lacey.

Visit WWW.LISASTACKPOLE.COM and click the "EMAIL US FOR GIVE-AWAYS" link to join our mailing list and sign up for contests!

Dr. Sydney,
Thank you for being here for me and my pack to help us lovingly honor Tucker Stackpole the Parti toy poodle with a heart of gold. Lisa Stackpole

Made in the USA
Columbia, SC
27 December 2019